THE HORSE
COMES FIRST

THE
HORSE
COMES FIRST

Mary Calhoun

Drawings by John Gretzer

Atheneum 1974 New York

To Anne and Hiram,
in memory of county fair days

Copyright © 1974 by Mary Calhoun
All rights reserved
Library of Congress catalog card number 73-84822
ISBN   0-689-30132-4
Published simultaneously in Canada by McClelland & Stewart, Ltd.
Manufactured in the United States of America
by Quinn & Boden Company, Inc.
Designed by Nancy Gruber
First Edition

Acknowledgment

I am grateful to the many harness horse owners, trainers and drivers who shared their knowledge and enthusiasm with me, and I give special thanks to Carol Paris and Donald Smith.

1

HARNESS HORSES! BOY, THOSE TROTTERS AND pacers, they're the neatest, the most beautiful performers, the way they clip along in their controlled gait. And mainly Charlie Stride. I almost feel sick when I think about how he's going on living his daily life, and I'm not with him. Right now maybe he's working out on the track, swinging his legs along, *clop-clop*—and somebody else is driving him. I love that trotting horse better than I could love any brother. Ah, Charlie—It's like I'm hardly living now, back in Denver, going to school. Last summer with the horses was the real life, last summer with Charlie Stride.

I caught the fever for harness racing the summer before last, when Mom and I spent two days at the farm at Olden, Iowa. We were driving to Chicago to see some friends of hers, and Mom said she couldn't miss seeing her dad and her sister, Connie. Before that we hadn't been to the farm since I was a little kid, when Grandma Hartshaw was still alive. Anyway, while we were there, a race meet was held at the Olden track. That was my first time at the races, and what a sight! Those beautiful horses racing around the track, tails streaming out, they were like horses flying against the sky when they were opposite us in the backstretch . . . like flying horses pulling chariots. There was a close field of them, all pulling sulkies and their drivers, and one of the drivers was my grandfather. I looked at that, and I knew there wasn't any more exciting or beautiful sight in the world.

I was hooked. Back in Denver that fall, even with all the newness—and nervousness—of going into junior high, seventh grade, I kept asking Mom, "Hey, why couldn't I spend next summer with Grandad and Aunt Connie?"

Then, late in September, a letter came from Aunt Connie, and that just whetted my appetite, because her letter read like a diary of her summer's racing adventures. She wrote,

After the races at Olden, we went to Mount Oak, were 3–4. On to Hooper, I was beaten by ½ nose in a blinding rainstorm, settled for second. They used a sweat scraper to get the mud off me. On to Bottville, Mo., starting gate broke down, and we went without the gate. I got away real good, but ran out of whammee! We were 5–5. By the way, it was 105° F., and the water

4

was so bad neither horse nor man could drink it, a good Pepsi day. On to Davenport, Ia., a long pull and rained us out. On to State Fair at Des Moines—100° F.—sunburned, finished 2–2. This was my fastest trip, 2:07. Great thrill. The other woman driver was in this race and won it. She made the remark the men were chasing us for a change! Anyway, Scataway paid for himself and all his expenses that trip.

It surprised me that a woman would actually be driving in races, and it isn't usual, but Aunt Connie seemed more like a man, anyway, so I didn't let that bother me.

All winter, the more I read the letter the more I got fired up about harness racing. I kept on asking Mom if I could go to Olden. Finally in the spring, when she found out she'd be away on some buying trips this summer, she said OK. Since the divorce, Mom has worked for a big furniture store in Denver, and at last she's working up as an interior decorating consultant and buyer. So Mom wrote to Grandad and arranged it, and all the rest of the spring I went around with a good feeling.

I got a book on harness horses and learned all about how they run in a gait, pacing or trotting, and have to win the race without breaking the gait. I read about the old famous racers: Greyhound, who held the trotting record for years; and Dan Patch, who used to ride around in his own railroad car with his picture painted on it. And about the great races on the Grand Circuit in the nineteenth century. A lot of people might think we'd left the harness racing sport back in the nineteenth century, a historical thing in the Currier and Ives prints. A lot of people in the West don't know anything but quarter horses, cowboy horses. But I knew about Messenger, the founding sire of the great Standardbred strain of harness horses, right after the Revolutionary War. I felt as if I was going around school with secret knowledge, and it made me feel great.

Then I got to Olden, and Grandad acted as if I didn't know anything. Which is probably true, but I felt just rotten at the time—for a long time.

It was the middle of June when I traveled to Olden, Iowa. On the train I was so excited I could hardly sleep, and in the morning I couldn't sit still in my seat. I kept getting up and walking to the water cooler, to the washroom, to the dome car to see the early morning Iowa hill country. All I could think about was, Boy, a whole summer of going around to county fairs and getting acquainted with the horses. And my grandfather—getting acquainted with my grandfather. I was so *up,* early that morning, and so *down* by night.

Things started going downhill the minute I stepped off the train. Wow, I couldn't believe how hot and humid it was in Iowa, after the air-conditioned train. The air smothered me like a hot, wet washrag, and I started sweating. I looked around the platform, spotted Grandad Hartshaw, and I really looked at him, the man I was going to spend the summer with. He's not very tall, kind of square and sandy haired, about as unexciting looking as a haystack—and that's the way his personality struck me, too, very low-key. He smiled, shook my hand, and said, "Good to see you, Randy." For Grandad, that was a great big greeting, flags flying, bands playing, because he's a very calm unemotional man. But I was all keyed up, and I started talking enough for both of us, asking how many horses did he have now (five), and when was the first race (next week), and could I go (maybe). That stopped me for a minute, that "maybe," because I'd just assumed I'd go everywhere with Grandad and Aunt Connie. Very much I wanted to be with my grandfather. Mom's great, but we'd had several years of just the two of us, and I wanted to be around a man, talk men's talk and stuff.

Well, I picked up my suitcase and followed Grandad, watching how he walked, kind of stumping along and limping just a little. I wondered if he had some old racing injury. When we got to where he'd parked the pickup truck, that was really neat, because I saw the cab door was lettered BELLEVIEW RACING STABLES, G. & C. HARTSHAW, OLDEN, IOWA. It made me feel special as we got into the truck. Grandad might look like a stumpy old farmer, but we were racing people, and everybody could see it.

The train had stopped at Trumbell, a trade-center

town about twenty miles from Olden. Grandad had a few errands, so that by the time he'd picked up groceries and some tools and stuff, it was noon when we headed out a narrow concrete road for Olden. As Aunt Connie hadn't come to town, I assumed she was at the farm cooking a big welcome dinner for me. I was really hungry, had my mouth all set for good old country cooking, homemade biscuits, maybe, and lashings of milk gravy.

Grandad didn't have much to say as he drove around town and went into stores, so I supposed he had his mind on his errands. I thought, That's OK, we'll get started when we get out on the road, then we'll start talking and getting acquainted. The summer before I hadn't had any chance alone with him. But no, we headed out of town, and still nothing. Grandad just sat up stocky to the wheel and steered the truck, sucking his teeth a little. It wasn't that he was unfriendly, exactly, but he certainly wasn't a man to make casual conversation. I asked a lot of questions, and he answered, "Yep," "Nope," until I began to feel edgy. I like to talk, sure, but I like people to talk back to me, be friends. Only twice did Grandad volunteer anything. Once he nodded toward a field, saying, "Good stand of hay there." And once he said, not looking at me, "See you got your father's red hair." That made me feel more nervous, because I'd gathered from Mom that Grandad didn't think much of Dad since he'd gone off and remarried.

Still, I wasn't really worried. I thought, OK, he's a quiet farmer type; it'll take a little time for us to get going.

I was looking forward to seeing Aunt Connie. The summer before I'd liked her, what little I'd seen of her. She'd seemed a little brusque, but she had sparkling brown eyes, and she reminded me of a leather strap, as lean and as strong. Maybe I liked her because she had kidded around with me a little after the races, when we were all excited about Grandad's win. Later, driving on to Chicago, I asked Mom how come Connie never got married, and Mom said Connie just never cared about anything but horses. She's quite a bit younger than Mom, about thirty, and there weren't any brothers to help Grandad with the farm and the horses, so Mom said Connie just naturally got into the horse business.

When Grandad drove into the farmyard, Aunt Connie came out the kitchen door, looking little and lean in dirty jeans. She gave me a big grin and hello:

"Hi! Good to see you! Come on in!"

I grinned, too, feeling welcome at last, thinking, Yeah! This is the way it should be, now we're really moving.

But then everything fell flat again. Aunt Connie had dinner on the kitchen table, so we sat right down to eat, and this is what we ate: thawed-out hero sandwiches, watery instant mashed potatoes, home-canned green beans, and bowls of store-canned peaches. The meal was watery and tasteless, as if

Aunt Connie didn't care whether I'd come or not. Even I fell silent for awhile as I began to eat that big disappointment of a meal. Then I saw Aunt Connie watching me, so I began chattering to her about how glad I was to come and how I wanted to drive a horse and how I hoped to be a big help with the horses.

She only said in a low calm voice, "We'll see. Better go slow at first."

She didn't smile. It didn't take me long to realize that Aunt Connie didn't grin often, although she's got a good grin. And she didn't talk lightly in conversation, throwing out ideas, any better than Grandad. During dinner we'd keep making starts. She and Grandad asked me a few things like the news about my mom and a polite question about what I'd been doing in school. I'd answer and run on until I could hear myself talking, so I'd stop, and then we'd fall silent again. In the silence I could hear flies buzzing in the kitchen and the clatter of dishes on the enameled table and the noise of my fork scraping on my plate. It all felt so awkward. I wondered what was the matter with them, what I'd done wrong. If I hadn't been eating, I would have chewed my fingernails.

Finally I thought, Well, there's still the horses, and I asked, "When can I see the horses?"

"Later," was all Grandad said.

I gave up pushing. The lack of talk in my Hartshaw relatives was beginning to stop even me.

Then, after dinner, nothing happened, either. Grandad said he had office work, and Aunt Connie drifted off, saying something about a nap. They just went off and left me alone. That was the end of my big beautiful welcome to the farm.

I thought, OK, be like that!

I decided I'd find the horses by myself. I went out to look around the farm, and that was another surprise, because the place seemed empty. The summer before I hadn't paid much attention to the farm, because we were busy with visitors dropping in and then going to the races, so I was still remembering it the way I'd seen it when I was five years old. Then Grandma Hartshaw had put cookies in my hands, and she'd taken me around to see everything. Then it had been a big bustling farm, with pigs, chickens, horses and machinery all over and a big vegetable garden on the other side of the house—every little kid's dream of a farm.

All gone. The place seemed deserted. No vegetable garden, no pigs in the sheds anymore, no horses in the barn, no chickens in the chicken houses, where Grandma used to preside over that operation. Especially no horses. I looked all over, and I couldn't find them anywhere.

I thought, Come on, they've got to be somewhere. What have they done with the horses?

I remember how I stood still there in the empty farmyard, trying to figure it out. The place was so quiet I could hear flies buzzing in the heat of the afternoon. Beyond the fences, on each side of the farm, acres of field corn stood stock-still, as if the corn had never rustled in a breeze. Nothing moved but the flies in that hot deserted place. The atmosphere was so heavy after the high dry air of Colorado that for a moment I wished I were back in Denver, where I could see the mountains rearing up, instead of flat miles of corn.

It was a lousy feeling—the watered-down dinner, the lonely empty mood of the farm, the way my relatives just left me alone—it was a wide letdown. Some start to my big summer with the horses.

But who wants to be gloomy? To fight the feeling, I started to climb the old wooden windmill.

Then, at last, Grandad came out of the house and called to me. He said, "Come on, Randy. Let's go to town and feed the horses."

Boy, did I come zipping down the rungs of that windmill!

"Town?" I asked.

"Sure," Grandad said, kind of grinning, "farmer lives on the farm, and the racehorses live in town."

Aunt Connie came out, and we went in the pickup truck, all three of us crowded into the seat. At last things were perking up, when it was a matter of the Hartshaws heading for their horses. I was out of my lousy mood right away—if I'd been a little kid, I'd have been bouncing on the seat. I was hoping Grandad would let me try driving a horse. I kept chewing my fingernails and then humming to keep from chewing, the way I do. And talking, of course.

Finally Aunt Connie told me, "Calm down. The horses won't like you if you come at 'em all tense like that."

We didn't have far to go. The farm is only a few miles from Olden, which is just a little country town, hardly a thousand people. However, Olden is the county seat, so the biggest layout there, besides the courthouse, is the county fairground—grandstand, barns and oval racetrack. That's where the Hartshaws keep their horses, in the barns, handy to the track for training. The summer before I hadn't realized the horses lived at the track, because the races were happening when I visited, and in fact, I hadn't gotten to see the horses up close, because Mom was in a rush to get out of the traffic after the races. In fact, living in the city, I had never been up close to any horse.

All that first day I'd been itching to get started. Well, once we got to the barns, things started happening fast enough, so fast that I got to meet only one of the Hartshaw horses. And that one meeting was a disaster.

At one side of the racetrack there were several long barns. We parked and went into one of the barns. It was shady and cooler in there under the high ceiling, and the place smelled of manure and dust and straw, a good smell. But mostly my first impression was: Wow, the place is full of life, horse life! The center of the barn was a broad passageway with

13

stalls lining each side, and there was a horse in nearly every stall. Down the line, horses put their heads out over the stall gates to look at us, horses whinnied to us, horses snorted. Toward the middle of the barn a horse was kicking and whanging against his stall, but then he stuck his head over the gate and gave us a high clear neigh of greeting.

"Hey, neat!" I yelled, starting to run toward that horse. "Hey, Grandad, which ones are yours?"

Grandad said, "Ssh! Quiet down!"

But he must have been feeling proud and happy to introduce his best horse to his only grandson, because he went on talking in a way that for him was breezy.

He said, "All right, Randy Meister, walk on down here and take a look at this old lady. This here is Miss Loubelle D., two, six!"

The "D." was for Direct, out of the great Direct line of horses, and those numbers were her mark, her best racing time, two minutes, six seconds to run a mile, although I didn't know what Grandad was talking about at the time. I only understood that he was proud of his horse and wanted to share her with me, so that made me feel good.

The first I saw of Miss Loubelle D. was her long gray nose hanging out over the stall gate and her dark eyes, gravely watching us approach. Some of the other horses were stamping around in their stalls like wild things, but Miss Loubelle D. stood quietly waiting for us to come to her, like a queen. She was a beauty, all right. Her head was sleek as old polished silver, and her mane contrasted darker, like shining tarnish. Miss Loubelle D. is a gray, which you don't often see on the racing circuit, most of the Standardbred horses being brown—bays. However, I remembered reading about the great Greyhound, so I wasn't surprised at her color. Her neat ears pricked forward as I hurried up to her. In the background I heard Grandad warn me to go slow. I was moving fast, and her nostrils flared, checking my smell, I realize now. I reached to smooth the beautiful gray horse's nose, but she moved her head aside from my hand, snorting a little and stamping. Then I saw there was an awful lot of horse back in that stall. And I mean *awful*—awesome.

"Here, let me take her out, so you can see her better," Grandad said. "You'll never see a prettier gray than Miss Loubelle D.!"

I stood back with Aunt Connie while Grandad unhooked the stall gate and led the mare out into the passageway. Since I'd never been around horses before, it really startled me how big and powerful a horse seems up close. Miss Loubelle D. was a lot of body moving and legs reaching out and feet going *clop* on the dirt. Hearing another horse kicking in his stall and seeing the gray moving, I realized all of a sudden that horses weren't quite the tame animals I'd vaguely thought. Ah, I don't know—maybe I was scared—a little. Still, Miss Loubelle D. was Grandad's pride, so I reached out to smooth her nose.

It was then that everything happened so fast. Miss Loubelle D. stepped on my foot. I smacked her face. And Grandad knocked me down.

Even now I don't know how I managed to get myself stepped on. Walk around behind a horse and get kicked, yes. Even smart horse people do that sometimes. But I came right up in front of that mare and got walked on. She wasn't trying to paw at me, she was just moving. Still, I was nervous, and suddenly there was a lot of power coming down on me, and I just struck out in split-second instinct. Next instant something hit my shoulder, and I was stretched on my stomach on the dirt.

Grandad said, "Don't ever do that again!"

Even then he didn't yell. His voice was flat as the side of an ax coming against my head.

I lay there in the dirt and straw, hearing Miss Loubelle's hooves clopping as Grandad led her back into the stall. He was talking to her softly. Aunt Connie hadn't made a sound. I scrambled myself up and ran out of the barn as fast as I could go, head down, stumbling.

There was nobody around but an old liver-colored hound dog. He nosed up to me, but I ran over behind the pickup truck and leaned my head against it, breathing hard. Then the breathing began to jerk, and I cried. I can't remember when I've cried since I was a little kid, but I cried then, and I remember the feel of my forehead pressed against the hot metal door of the truck. The tears came spurting out like I was trying to wash down the truck. Then I heard Aunt Connie's voice, and I panicked. I thought, She's not seeing me like this, and I'm not riding back in the truck with them, either. I couldn't stand that, sitting up close between them, and them not talking to me.

So I started running back to the farm. At least I could find the way, because we'd driven straight down the gravel road from the farm to the fairground on the edge of town. I walked or ran all the way, and I don't remember anything I saw of the countryside that day. When I got to the farm, I was beat. My foot hurt, too, the one the horse had stepped on. I went up to the room they'd said was to be mine, and flopped down on the bed. I just lay there for maybe an hour, chewing my fingernails, and wondering what kind of a man was he, to sock his grandson, and thinking maybe I should go back to Denver and wondering how I could get to the train on my own. I was just realizing that, whatever, I'd have to apologize to Grandad, when I heard the pickup drive in.

It hadn't occurred to me that they might worry where I'd gone. Grandad's feet clomped into the kitchen, and he shouted, "Randy? Are you here?" I lay on the bed a second, wondering just how mad he was. Then I came out to the head of the stairs and said, "Yeah, I'm here. Look, I'm sorry about the horse. When she stepped on me, I just struck out without—"

"Get down here," he said.

I got down there.

Then he sat me down at the kitchen table, and to my surprise, Grandad talked to me very quietly about horses and how you treat them. I didn't take in much of what he said; I was just grateful that he didn't whale away at me, because I didn't know what to expect from a silent man like him. But when he kept going on, so cool and matter of fact about the way to treat horses, I began to see he wasn't thinking about me, at all. I thought he was full of distaste for me, and therefore he was concentrating on the horse part of it.

I can't stand for people not to like me. Maybe it's weak of me, but I just can't stand it, and I find myself doing all kinds of crazy things to get people to like me. So I started talking a lot to Grandad, trying to explain. "A dumb reflex reaction," I said, "but I like horses better than almost anything, and I'll never do a thing like that again." And so on.

No beautiful rapport with my grandfather resulted from my efforts. He quit talking and started to eat the food Aunt Connie had been setting on the table. I felt so low I don't even remember what it was. All that time Aunt Connie hadn't said anything, but she smiled at me once.

After supper I carried the dishes to the sink and found the dish towel. I always help Mom with the dishes after dinner, and I wanted to try again to make friends with Aunt Connie. Grandad had gone outside, so we were alone in the kitchen.

"Is the horse all right?" I asked. "I didn't really hurt her, did I?" Until then I hadn't given a thought to that part of it.

Aunt Connie wasn't quite as reassuring as I'd expected. She said very seriously that it could have been bad if I'd scratched Miss Loubelle D.'s eyes, but that the mare seemed to be all right.

She washed the glasses and cups without saying anything, and then she added, "You'll have to approach Miss Loubelle D. very carefully after this. She won't forget you hit her."

Geez! I thought. Then the trouble isn't over?

"You mean she may try to kick me, try to get revenge?" I asked.

"No. Oh well, she might, but I doubt that. She's a very calm horse," Aunt Connie said. "What I mean is, you've got an uphill climb to get her to like you."

I felt rotten. It looked to me as if things had been downhill all the way, ever since I stepped off the train.

"What about Grandad?" I asked bitterly. "Does he hate me, too?"

She glanced up at me, then gave a little snort down toward the dishpan. "Huh. He doesn't know you well enough to hate you."

After that, I couldn't say anything. I hadn't really thought the horse was hurt bad or that my grandfather would hate me, but—geez!

Aunt Connie went on washing the dishes, and then she started talking. "All right, Randy, I'm going to tell you something, and you just keep it under your hat, what I tell you. There's a man named Jake Bottle who races horses. He's been around on the circuit for quite a few years, and we've gotten to know him pretty well, one way or another. He's a mean man, and he's mean with his horses. He punches them with his fists."

"Huh?" I stared at her.

"Jake Bottle wants to win," she said. "Sure, we all do, but with that man it's just business. He wants to win the races for the sake of the purse money. So if a horse of his doesn't run well or breaks stride during a race, Jake beats up his horse when he gets it back to the barn. I've seen him."

"But—" I couldn't make that jibe. "You said I'd have a long way to go with Miss Loubelle D. How can this man handle his horses if he's always slapping them around?"

Aunt Connie scrubbed a pot for a long time. At last she said, "Jake is strong-willed. Maybe he's got his horses broken to his will." And then, grudgingly, "Oh, I suppose he likes horses in his own way, or he wouldn't be in the business." She dumped out the dishwater and faced around to me.

"Anyway, Dad despises that man for the way he treats his horses. So don't you dare shape up like Jake Bottle!"

Boy! If I'd worked at it, I couldn't have found anything more exactly wrong to do, my first day in Olden, than to hit Grandad's favorite horse.

I told Aunt Connie, "Believe me, the last thing in the world I want to do is go around hitting horses!"

She nodded. "OK. It was a bum start, but we'll get over it."

She went outdoors. I'd had enough of trying to make friends with anybody in Olden, so I wandered into the front room, turned on the TV set and slumped down to watch it. Aunt Connie and Grandad didn't come in, so after one show I went up to get ready for bed. By that time I was more mad than anything else. It just didn't seem fair. Grandad acted as if he didn't care whether I was there or not, maybe rather not. His only grandson, you'd think he'd be glad I'd come to spend the summer. Instead, he acted about as excited as if he'd found a worm in his soup. He was about as interested in me as he would be in a shadow on the wall.

It really hurt. Sure, I'd been excited about a summer of horses and races, thinking that's why I'd come. But deep down what I really wanted was my grandfather, to get to know him and for him to like me. A man. My parents were divorced when I was seven. At first Dad would take me places on Saturdays, but then he moved back to Seattle and got married again, and I haven't seen him since. My Meister grandparents live in Seattle, so that I hardly remember them. I hadn't seen much of Mom's folks, either —after the divorce I think she was embarrassed to come back to the farm—but I'd gotten the impression that Grandad Hartshaw was a solid friendly man, the few times I'd seen him, and I'd really been looking forward to being around him all summer.

I remember that first night, lying there in my bed staring around at the bare bedroom. Even though it was a hot summer night, the room struck me as cold and bare, because there was hardly anything in it, just the bed and dresser and a cheap throw rug on the floor by the bed. I was used to wall-to-wall shag carpeting in our apartment and Mom's decorating effects. At Olden the whole farmhouse seemed as stripped down and cheerless as the bedroom, with old linoleum on the floors everywhere, even the front room, and just a few pieces of stuffy uncomfortable furniture. The bare house, the empty farm—it seemed a place that was hardly lived in.

I thought, Maybe Grandad didn't want me to come. After all, he didn't ask me; he's never asked me to come, all these years. I should go back to Denver. I'm sure not going to hang around here where nobody gives a damn about me.

Then I heard Grandad and Aunt Connie come into the kitchen below from outdoors. I heard their voices, and they were talking about me. I sat up in bed to listen. It was crazy, but all of a sudden I felt better, because at least they were talking about me, thinking about me.

"—good kid," Aunt Connie was saying. "He's sure friendly enough. Reminds me of a pup rushing around, knocking things over with his tail, wagging it so hard."

"Huh. More like a tornado," Grandad said.

There was a silence, then a rustle of newspaper. I listened for Grandad to say something more. Finally he did.

"Give him time," he said. "He's a Hartshaw. We'll gentle him."

I let out my breath and lay back down. I wasn't sure I wanted to be gentled, but it sounded as though Grandad accepted me as his, one of his own. Maybe we'd get something good going between us, after all. I went right to sleep that first night without worrying about strange night sounds in the country.

2

THEN THE NEXT DAY I FELL IN LOVE WITH A HORSE.
It was worth going through the misery of that first
day to come to that fine second day, because that was
the day I met Charlie Stride. Of course, not everything about the day was so great, but nothing can
ever take away the feeling I had the first time I drove
Charlie.

It was so early the next morning, when I heard
sounds down in the kitchen, that all the birds were
still squeaking away in the big trees around the farmhouse. I got into my clothes and hurried downstairs
to see what was happening. Halfway down, though,
I slowed on the narrow stairs and started biting my
fingernails, wondering how Grandad would treat me
after the trouble the day before.

However, he said pleasantly enough, "Morning!
How'd you sleep?"

He and Aunt Connie were standing in the kitchen,

24

drinking cups of coffee, and there was no sign of breakfast preparations. Aunt Connie handed me a glass of milk and told me to drink up and come along with them.

"First we tend to the horses, then we'll get some breakfast," she said.

I thought, Neat enough! As I gulped down the milk, I remembered Miss Loubelle D.

"Horses like sugar, don't they?" I said to Aunt Connie. "Do you have a lump of sugar I could take to Miss Loubelle D.?"

She looked at me over the coffee cup. "Sure. Smart kid," she said, so that made me feel good, too. She reached in the cupboard and handed me three lumps of sugar, saying, "If you want the horses to like you, remember we've got three horses."

Grandad added, "Got more than that. Did you see Miss Maybelle and her foal yesterday afternoon?"

He was nice and cheerful, not seeming to worry anymore about my trouble the day before. I thought maybe he was a morning person and talked more in the mornings. Me, I'm ready anytime. At first I only registered that Grandad was being friendly to me, but then I caught the part about the horses.

I said, No, where were they? I'd looked all over the farm for horses.

"Out in the pasture behind the barn, the part that goes down into the woods," he told me. "Maybe they were down at the creek when you looked. Anyways, they're out there prancing fancy this morning."

"Hey, I want to see them!" I was already heading for the back door, but Grandad caught me by the arm.

"Hold up, fireball," he said. "We've got to go to town. You can see Miss Maybelle this afternoon."

"Yeah," Aunt Connie said, rinsing out her cup, "that Scataway will be stomping his stall if I don't get in there and feed him."

So we all climbed into the pickup truck to head for the horse barns, and I felt great: now we were moving together. However, I pushed it too far, and I guess I was being fakey, too, trying to make up to Grandad. Because I started talking a lot of blow about what a beautiful horse Miss Loubelle D. was and how I could just tell she must be a great racer. Huh, I'm embarrassed for the kid I was. Grandad didn't answer, just whistled in a silent hissing way through his teeth.

So I switched to asking questions, and I did find out one thing: why the farm was so stripped down, no more big operation of farming, or pigs and chickens. Grandad had leased out most of his land.

"Got enough money now," he said. "Don't need to do that anymore."

And Aunt Connie said, "Why waste time feeding pigs and chickens, when you can be working with horses?"

I remember those statements, because that's about all I got out of them except for "Yup" and "Uh-huh." Grandad did say, "Still raise my own oats," but that didn't mean anything to me at the time. However, I began to understand the picture, and it fit along with the bare house and scanty meals. Grandad and Aunt Connie didn't waste time on anything that didn't have to do with their horses. They were like athletes in training for the Olympics, all headed in just one way. I'd never known anybody so one direction, and I felt in awe of them, maybe even a little afraid. I started to say something, but Aunt Connie cut me off.

"Now listen to me, Randy. There's one important thing about horses."

I checked that she'd used my name and smiled at her, then I paid attention to what she was saying, which is a good thing.

"Touch and sounds," she was saying. "A horse gets to know you by your touch and by the sounds you make."

It's hard to realize, Aunt Connie said, how sensitive a horse is to touch and how much of his world a horse takes in through his ears. She told how she treats a foal, getting it accustomed to her by gently running her hand along its back, squatting down to the foal's size, picking up its feet—because a horse has to get used to having its feet handled—and talking softly to the young animal.

So, she said, I shouldn't go into the barns all jittery and yelling, "Hey, neat." If I did, I'd only make the horses nervous about me. "A calm steady hand, that's what a horse responds to," she said.

Grandad grunted, "Um," nodding his head a little.

OK, I thought. Easy does it, steady on. But we were pulling up to the barn by then, and I heard a horse neighing, and I felt nervous and excited, anyway.

I had intended to go first to Miss Loubelle D. with a lump of sugar. Instead, as we walked down the center aisle of the barn, a brown horse whinnied at me. It was that same clear neigh I'd heard the day before, the same horse who'd been rattling his stall. He put his long brown face over the stall gate just as I went by, and bobbed his head up and down, giving a happy whinny, exactly as if he was saying, "Hello, Randy, glad to see you!" His ears pricked forward, and his big brown eyes looked at me, not at my aunt or Grandad.

"Ahhh," I went softly, remembering what Aunt Connie had said about voices, and I put my hand very gently but steadily on the horse's head. His hair felt like soft thin paper laid right over the bones of his skull. He was a light bay horse, a rich brown that stopped just short of being reddish, and he had a neat black mane. He twitched his nostrils, smelling me, and then he butted his nose against my chest. Boy, did I like that! It was friendly, the way he butted me, like "Hey, we're just a couple of kids, let's wrestle!" If I'd had any twinges before about being afraid of horses, I got over them right then.

"Want something, fella?" I said. "Try this." I held a lump of sugar in my hand under his nose. Wow,

"See you later, fella," and then moved on with Grandad to the next stall.

Miss Loubelle D. was watching us over the gate, and I felt nervous again, as I wondered whether she remembered that I'd hit her. I think she did, because she pulled back her head when I came near and stared at me, flicking her ears.

I asked Grandad, "Does she hate me?"

That made him mad, I guess, because he said, ry strongly, "Miss Loubelle D.? Why, she doesn't ow what hate is! She's the calmest steadiest horse e ever known. Quit talking like that!"

Miss Loubelle D. didn't look calm to me. She was king her sleek gray head, and she rolled her eyes he white showed. I wasn't entirely sure she dn't bite me, but I put another lump of sugar on and and held it up toward her mouth. I made nd and my voice steady, saying, "I'm sorry, oubelle D."

mare stopped shaking her head and watched eyes dark and quiet then, and I waited. She t my hand, and I tried to hold it firm when th came down. She lipped up the sugar. She t, working her mouth around, showing her then she snorted, *"Whup-up-up."*

hat mean she likes me?" I asked Grandad.

e a little snort of his own, "Huh," and is shoulders. But anyway, that much went ith Miss Loubelle D., although I didn't ld venture to pat her yet.

that felt neat, when his lips worked on
gathering up the lump. I didn't know a ho
could feel so soft. I could respond to
touch, too. I watched him chew up
course, a horse can't smile, but if
grinned at me, that brown one did, w
smacking his lips.

It seems funny now that when I
Stride, all I got acquainted with w
in the stall was all the rest of the h
legs and haunches that made a
the moment all I saw was hi
enough. Right away I saw that
was just as ready to be frien

All that time, Grandad a
said a thing. Finally I beca
ing there silently, watching
I looked around, Grandad

He said, "That there is
ful colt I ever saw. But
own way. He might ma
him settled down."

Aunt Connie pa
"He's a two-year-ol
racing season this su

Then he was o
several other hors
horses, so it coul
belonged to so
smooth down

Meanwhile, there'd been some snorting and stomping around in the stall across the way, and Aunt Connie was saying, "Ho! Whoa, man!" Then she led a dark brown horse out into the middle of the barn.

She said proudly, "This is my horse. This is Scataway."

Scataway was a bay, too, but such a dark brown he was almost black, and he looked like a lot of high-spirited horse for little Aunt Connie to be handling, the way he tossed himself around and snorted. I could just imagine those prancing legs flicking in a race—or kicking. However, in no time my aunt had him fastened to the crossties in the passageway between the stalls, and she started to wipe him down. I turned to come up behind them, but Aunt Connie said, "Look out! He's spooky."

"Do you mind if I watch?" I asked.

However, Grandad gave his little snort again, saying, "Watch, nothing. Let's get to work."

So, work we did. Or Grandad did. Mostly all I did was stumble around, get in the way, and do things wrong. Now it seems so simple: first thing in the morning you clean up the horses and their stalls and feed the horses. But that day I slopped water all down the middle of the barn when I filled the bucket too full at the faucet. I threw Scataway's hay on the floor of his stall before we'd forked out the old straw and manure. I ran up in front of Scataway, making him jump back almost onto Aunt Connie.

At that, Grandad snapped, "Quit running around like a chicken with its head off, or get out of here."

I thought, gee, what a grouch.

But I sure didn't want to stay out of the barn. Charlie Stride was chewing on the wire fastening his stall gate, as if he could hardly wait to get out, and I'd been giving him a pat as I went by, hurrying like crazy to get done so I could spend some time with him, get more acquainted. I wanted to ride that brown colt. I thought if I could feel him between my legs, be a part of him when he moved, then we'd start to know each other.

So I told Grandad, "I'm sorry."

While this was going on, a heavyset younger man had come into the barn and was taking care of his horses. I saw him grinning at me and Grandad.

He said, "Morning, George. Who's your new groom?"

"My grandson."

I thought Grandad wasn't going to say anymore. I thought maybe it was embarrassing for him to admit, This dumb kid running around like a chicken with its head off is my one and only neat grandson. But his face didn't show anything, and after a few-beat pause he added,

"Randy Meister, meet Boyd Gray."

We said "Hello," and the man, still grinning, went into a stall with a can of oats.

I felt burned. It seemed as though everything I'd done since I'd come to Olden was off-balance, everybody thought I was a fool.

I said again to Grandad, "Look, I'm sorry!"

He had Miss Loubelle D. out of her stall, fastening her to the crossties, and he didn't look at me, but he said, "Don't know much about horses, do you?"

Geez, I thought he could have realized that and made allowances. "No," I said, just level, "living in the city, I don't know much about horses."

He glanced at me then, and I saw I'd scored.

"Want to learn?" he asked.

"Yes! Of course," I said. "That's why I came to Olden."

"All right," he said, "the first thing you need to know—first, last and always—is this: The horse always comes first."

I nodded and waited for the next lesson. But there wasn't any next statement. Grandad started wiping down Miss Loubelle D. After awhile he handed me a brush and told me to curry her haunches. Of course, I didn't do it right—at first I was standing off from her, in case she tried to kick me, and next I got to admiring the dark dapple swirls in her gray hair and rubbed her hair the wrong way—and then I found out Grandad had expected me to watch exactly how he curried horses. Lessons were going to be mostly "show" and very little "tell." That bugged me a little, that he'd caught me that way, because I never have been a great one for detail.

At last when my stomach thought it must be nearly noon, and the horses were eating contentedly,

Aunt Connie said, "OK, let's go get some breakfast."

Actually, we'd been at the barn only about an hour, and I suppose my fooling around had taken up time, because other mornings those chores went faster. We ate at a little diner near the fairground, and I couldn't believe it when I saw the diner clock registering only 7:15. After we'd eaten, we went back to the barn, and then the best part of the morning came, working out the horses.

When we walked into the barn, I could hear Charlie Stride whickering softly. I saw that the colt was reaching his head down toward a fluffy yellow cat, which was smoothing up against the stall gate.

Aunt Connie gave a little "huh" chuckle, saying, "That Charlie talks to everybody."

Grandad led the colt out of his stall, fastened him to the crossties, and began putting the harness on him. I thought I'd better watch closely how he did it. When Grandad put the bit in Charlie's mouth, the horse began chewing on it with a clicking sound. Why? I asked.

"Ah, he's always a-wallering his tongue," Granddad said. "Just a nervous habit."

That made me laugh. I thought, Sure, because he can't chew his fingernails!

"You and me, Charlie," I whispered, smoothing his nose and neck, reaching up to scratch behind his ears. He went *"Whuff-uff,"* nodding his head. He lipped at my arm, maybe looking for more sugar. But

I could tell he liked me. He was just as frisky and eager for us to get together as I was.

While this love feast was going on, Grandad had brought up a jog cart. His hands worked so quickly and surely that I didn't realize what was happening until both of the poles were lashed into Charlie's harness.

"Hey!" I said, then cooling it, "Um—Grandad," I stuttered a little, "well, I was kind of hoping I'd get to ride Charlie Stride. Would there be any chance today?" I asked.

Grandad's chin jerked up at me as if he was mad, and maybe he was. "Are you nuts!" he exclaimed. I remember how funny "nuts" sounded, coming from an old farmer. He shook his head at what a dumb kid I was. He said mildly enough, "You're going the wrong route. You don't ride a horse like this. You drive him."

I tried, "I know, but I just thought—"

I came to a stop, because Grandad kept on looking at me, kind of studying me. Then he made the best offer I'd heard all morning.

He said, "I'll take Charlie Stride out, see how he's feeling today. You watch what I do. Then maybe you can drive him."

"OK!" I said.

Aunt Connie was harnessing Scataway ahead of us in the passageway. She said, "That colt's pretty undependable for a new kid to drive."

But Grandad said, "We'll see."

He helped her hitch another jog cart to Scataway. The cart was simply two wheels on an axle, with a seat in the middle. From the frame, long poles extended to hitch into the horse's harness, with a cross pole between them for the driver to brace his feet up on and a canvas apron hanging between the poles to keep mud from flying up into the driver's face from the horse's heels. I learned later that jog carts were only for working out the horses. In races the drivers rode on sulkies—"bikes," they call them—which are lighter and sit closer up to the horse.

Adjusting the poles into Scataway's harness, Aunt Connie told me, "Watch their legs when they run, see the difference. Charlie Stride is a trotter, and Scataway is a pacer." She added to Grandad, "Though I still think you should have switched Charlie to pace this spring. Be a lot easier, with him so feisty."

"Nope," Grandad said. "Charlie Stride's a trotter. Trot, that's all he wants to do. He'll make his speed, you watch."

I wondered if Grandad and Connie ever quarreled, strong-minded as they both seemed to be.

Then they led the horses out of the barn, swung onto the carts and headed through the gate onto the track, like a two-place parade. I leaned against the fence rail to watch. And what a sight that was to see! What a sweet morning! The air was balmy, smelling of grass and dust, and it was so quiet out there in the country at the track, with only the sounds of birds singing, the *clop-clop* of the horses' hooves and the whirr of the cartwheels. I remember mornings and mornings of watching at the fence rail and out on the track myself, but that was my first morning in the world for watching harness horses work out.

Glossy brown horse, shining dark horse, they ran with their heads held high, tails streaming out, legs moving in rhythm, not very fast, just an easy jog. It was more than seeing each horse, though, for there was a total event going by, horse, cart and driver; first Scataway and Aunt Connie, then Charlie Stride and Grandad. Beautiful! I watched how Grandad sat up, holding the reins, and I could hardly wait to get up on the cart behind Charlie myself.

I watched the horses' legs to see what they meant about gaits. At first Charlie's trotting gait looked complicated to me, but then I caught on: it was a diagonal gait. His left front leg and right rear leg moved forward as his opposite legs moved back. Whereas, Scataway, pacing, moved his right legs forward as the two legs on his other side were going back. Sidewheeling, they call it.

But Charlie, the trotter—oh, that was beautiful! As he came past me, he looked like a horse floating smoothly above the ground, with just his hooves coming down in rhythm to check the ground for balance. I could hear *clop-clop, clop-clop* in an exact two-beat, even though four hooves were striking the dirt. Maybe he was showing off for me, because he speeded up a little, and then as he went on around the track, my ears caught the wrong sound—*ker-clop, ker-clop*. Charlie had broken gait and was galloping. Immediately, Grandad sawed the reins back and forth. The colt didn't like that, and he danced around a little, almost rearing, but Grandad kept control of him. He stopped Charlie, started him again, and they went on, *clop-clop, whirr*. The next time they came around I heard Grandad humming easily, and I smiled. It was such a happy thing, there under the sun, horse doing his job properly, man holding the reins and humming at ease.

The track was a half-mile oval with fence all around it, and the Hartshaws took the horses around for several miles. Remembering that first jog training, I can go on and on thinking about it, but actually the horses were only out on the track for about ten minutes.

"Beautiful!" I called to Aunt Connie, as she drove off the track at a slow pace. "Just great!"

She grinned at me. "And you know why?" she said. "Because they were running in a schooled gait. You watch their legs? See Charlie break? A harness horse can't run hell-bent-for-leather, gallop to get there first, the way thoroughbreds do in running races. A harness horse has to get there first in his controlled gait, trot or pace. Now *that* takes a well-trained horse! That's what is beautiful about harness racing!"

Her voice rang. She was a truly happy woman.

"Yes!" I said, catching her happiness.

Even Grandad was smiling at me, smiling at the

world. However, the next thing on his schedule for me was work again.

I was saying, "Now can I—"

But he said, "Nope. Now Charlie's got to blow down. Later we'll go out. Now you can take care of him."

Well, taking care of Charlie wasn't work. While Grandad led Miss Loubelle D. out for her turn around the track, Aunt Connie showed me how to help with the hot horses. Both Charlie Stride and Scataway were sweaty with lather on their coats, so we wiped them down with cool water and gave them a little water to drink. Maybe it was then that Aunt Connie told me how to water a horse when he's really hot from racing, but I was busy talking to Charlie and listening to him *whuffle* to me. Next Aunt Connie rubbed some liniment on the horses' legs— "kind of an osteopathic treatment"—and then we put blankets on them and put them in their stalls to cool down. Charlie had to be tied by the head in his stall, because "he always chews his blanket."

Charlie Stride was beginning to remind me of a puppy, the way he chewed on things.

By then, Grandad was coming back with the gray mare, so I didn't get to see her jog that time. While we were waiting for the horses to cool down, Aunt Connie and I went out to the fence and watched the other man, Boyd Gray, giving his horse a workout. The horse was going lickety-cut around the track, and I worried that he had a faster horse than the

Hartshaws. But Aunt Connie said they'd only been jogging their horses, whereas Gray was taking his horse for a brush of top speed.

"See, he's going the right way around the track," she pointed out.

"When you're jogging a horse, you go the 'wrong' way around the track, clockwise," she explained. "Then when you want to ask a horse for speed, you turn him around and travel the 'right' way, counter-clockwise, the way you'd be going in a race. A horse soon learns he should lay on the steam when he's going the 'right' way," she said.

Gol! So many details about horses and racing that first day—I'd really come to a different world.

But the biggest thing I remember about that morning was a feeling thing, not a factual thing. I remember how it felt the first time I drove Charlie Stride.

Grandad came out of the barn with the brown colt already hitched to a jog cart, and said to me, "Come on."

"Now? Oh, wow!" I started to climb onto the cart.

But Grandad said, "Hold up. You don't know anything about driving horses. Get up here in front of me."

Geez! I had to drive Charlie while sitting on Grandad's lap like a baby! Of course, I didn't know the first thing about how a horse could act, and I could have fouled up a valuable horse, out there by myself. But I was burned, thinking Grandad didn't trust me.

Aunt Connie didn't help matters. She kind of chuckled, saying, "Jog carts aren't built for two," as we tried to get ourselves arranged on the cart. Grandad sat on the seat, with me hunched onto his lap, my feet braced out on the poles. Charlie kept looking back at our squirming around as if he couldn't believe it. We started off like an awkward mistake, Grandad extending his arms around me to hold the reins with one hand and touch the colt's haunches with the whip in his other hand. Then Grandad put the reins in my hands, and I forgot all about being mad or awkward.

I could feel Charlie Stride! I could feel the horse moving against the reins.

At first I let the reins go too slack, and immediately Charlie slowed almost to a stop.

"Pull the reins tight between you and him. He's got to feel the bit in his mouth," Grandad said. He touched the colt with the whip, talking to him, "Come on, Charlie, let's go. Yes, Charlie."

So I tightened up on the reins. We moved off around the track, speeding up just a little. And it was so great! Because the horse took hold of me. Through the reins I could feel his forward thrust and the movement of his body, so rhythmic. He was pulling me, but it wasn't a matter of pulling me off the cart. It was a matter of feeling the horse work, the reins like a bond between him and me.

"Wow!" I said softly.

I must have slacked the reins a little, because

Charlie Stride slowed, flicking his ears.

"Hold steady," Grandad told me. "Don't pull up too tight, that brings him down. But let him feel you holding him. He's balancing himself against the bit and the reins as he thrusts forward. Heeyuh, Charlie!" He flicked the whip lightly on the horse. "Come on! Feel how you and him balance against the reins when he speeds up?"

I could feel it. I was feeling Charlie through the reins, and he was feeling me, too. Ah, beautiful! There really was a solid team interaction between horse and driver!

I felt like singing my heart out, jogging along so smooth and easy with Charlie Stride, but I settled for humming, the way I'd heard Grandad doing. As we came to one of the turns, Grandad said Charlie was getting too far toward the inside, so to pull the left rein a little. I did, gently, and the horse responded exactly, a mild little turning, no sudden veering out.

And Grandad—I learned something new about him. For a nontalker, he was talking all the time to the horse: "All right, Charlie, take it easy on the turn. Come on, Charlie, let's go. That's the way, Charlie." Quiet easy talk, it was. Strangely, it was I who didn't have much to say, I was so absorbed in driving the horse.

And looking at him. It was a funny view of a horse, riding up behind him. The colt looked all wide haunches, hooves coming up backward and head beyond the body. A checkrein kept his head held up so

high. I could see his ears sticking up like signals. While we jogged, they were pricked forward, but Grandad said when a horse is really concentrating on racing fast, he lays his ears back.

Aunt Connie came around the track with Scataway, and she passed us, Scataway's heels flinging up bits of dirt. Maybe Charlie Stride didn't like to be passed, because he speeded up. The pull on the reins lifted me for a second, and we were sailing along, the horse's power coming right up through my arms.

"Slow, Charlie," Grandad said, and to me, "Loose up on the reins a fraction, eas-y."

I eased the reins, and instead of running faster, Charlie slowed a bit, his ears flicking as if listening for a message. He steadied into the slightly slower speed, his legs never breaking the trotting gait, and I held him with the reins at that speed. Oh yes, we were a team!

Then, when our rounds were done, and we slowly headed off the track, Grandad said, "Charlie horse don't always respond to the reins quite so neat. You must have caught the touch pretty good, buddy."

I could have fallen over with happiness. My shut-mouthed grandfather had actually spoken words of praise for me. It was like putting the stamp on it, that Charlie Stride and I were going to be a team.

I'm glad I had that one moment of pure happiness, because then it all fell apart.

Grandad said, "OK, buddy, he's all yours."

I thought he meant me, and I slid off his lap to go

take Charlie's bridle. I was seeing myself leading him off to his stall and telling him all about what a great couple we were going to be.

Instead, a girl took hold of the colt's bridle.

Grandad was saying, "Randy, meet Pen Greeley."

Pen. She was such a skinny stick of a girl, so colorless and nothing looking when I first saw her, to cause me so much grief last summer. She had a very ordinary face, long sandy hair tied back in two tails, and she was as tall as I was, although later I found out she was younger, twelve. She seemed shy, because she said "Hello" looking into Charlie's nose.

I looked a "What's this?" to Grandad, who was already unhitching the cart from Charlie's harness.

"Pen's been helping us with the horses for a couple years now," he said. "She can show you a lot."

Oh great, I thought. A girl who knows all about horses—and she saw me driving a horse from my grandpa's lap!

As Pen led Charlie Stride into the barn, Grandad pushed his chin in their direction, saying, "Go on, help her."

At that point I didn't realize how much a part of the Hartshaw setup Pen was. I just saw that some dumb girl was leading the colt away before I could sweet-talk with him about our trip around the track. I ran after them. Pen was leading Charlie Stride down the passageway, and I saw it. My horse, my buddy, was leaning his head down on that girl's shoulder, nuzzling her neck.

I stood there just inside the barn entrance, in the dark after all the sunlight outside, and I watched. The girl fastened Charlie into the crossties and began wiping him down, all the time talking to him in a sweet light voice, all about "How are you, Charlie? I'm sorry I was late today." And Charlie whinnied and whuffled softly to her.

I heard Grandad's voice again, saying, "helping us with the horses for a couple of years now," and it began to register. This girl was part of the "In" team. Grandad had called her "buddy." He expected us to become jolly playmates at taking care of the horses. Huh!

And double huh!

I walked down the passage and took the sponge out of the girl's hand. Without saying anything, I began to wipe Charlie down myself. She didn't speak, either. She looked at me, startled, stood there for a minute, then went to get Charlie's blanket. I let her stand by, holding the blanket, while I rubbed Charlie's nose.

Then I said to her, "You live in town?"

"No," she almost whispered. "On the farm next to the Hartshaws. We're neighbors."

That figured.

"Your folks got any horses?"

"No, that's why—" she whispered.

Yeah.

"You gonna be a big neat woman driver like Aunt Connie when you grow up?"

46

"I don't know." She said it looking into Charlie's blanket, then threw it over his back and led him into his stall.

Bluh, I thought. Great possibilities for a deep and lasting friendship with *that* girl! She didn't even have spunk enough to tease me about riding on my grandfather's lap. She had about as much depth as a piece of straw. She had about as much character as a bowl of oatmeal.

So why did Charlie Stride like her so well?

Just then Aunt Connie came into the barn leading Scataway after their workout. The dark horse was still prancing in a skittish way. Aunt Connie saw Pen coming out of the stall and me hanging up harness.

"Yeah, Randy," she called to me, "I thought you'd make friends with Pen, because she can show you a lot about horses. She's been training Charlie Stride since he was a pup. That colt follows Pen around as if she had him on a string."

I looked at my stupid aunt, and I could feel my face stiffening.

"Oh, yeah. Sure. Great," I said. I felt as if I might snarl next. Which was crazy, I realized, because Aunt Connie didn't know I'd fallen so hard for Charlie Stride.

I snatched on something to get myself back to facts and pointed to all the leather cage of harness Scataway was wearing around his legs, asking,

"Does he wear more harness than Charlie because Scataway is spooky?"

Laugh? Geez! Even now I don't think my question was that funny. But Aunt Connie burst out laughing, and I saw Pen grinning into a stall gate.

Burn!

No, Aunt Connie told me, when she finally got over her laughing fit, the leather "cage" was the hobbles, to keep Scataway in the pacing gait, to guide his legs.

But she and Pen, those two females, had to keep on giggling at the dumb kid from the city.

That was the second time I seriously considered going back to Denver.

But then I felt something nudging my shoulder, and I looked around right into Charlie Stride's brown eyes. I remembered how it felt when I'd driven him. I looked at Charlie, smoothing his nose, not paying anymore attention to the women, and I firmed up. So what if I was new to it all, new to this friendly horse. Charlie Stride was going to be my horse, and someday I'd drive him in a race.

3

GIRLS ARE ALL RIGHT. THERE WAS A GIRL AT SCHOOL
last year, Kaylee, whom I was very interested in, although she isn't back this year. But Pen didn't even
seem like a girl at first. At times she seemed like a
little kid, and at other times, like a small-sized quiet
adult. It wasn't that she was boyish, not tomboyish
like some girls I've known, the "Hey, pal, pitch it
over here!" kind. But she wasn't a feminine girl,
either, no softness or jingle about her. She was simply a twelve-year-old person who went about the
business of tending horses very matter of factly.

The first few days I tried to ignore Pen, hoping
she'd go visit an aunt in Ohio, or something. But although she was quiet, she was there at the barn every
morning. She rode her bicycle to the fairground, and
she'd usually be at the barn with Charlie Stride when
we came back from breakfast at the diner. Since she
lived on the next farm, I wondered why Grandad

didn't pick her up on the way to town, but then Aunt Connie mentioned that Pen had lots of brothers and sisters, and she had to help with the chores of a big family before she left home. I didn't find out much from Pen, because I didn't talk to her anymore than I had to. I have to really dislike a person not to talk—though I felt insulted one time when I heard Grandad say to Boyd Gray, "Randy talks as much as a hen that's just laid an egg."

I was jealous, of course. It was "Pen and Charlie —this" and "Pen and Charlie—that." From things the Hartshaws dropped, I learned it was Pen who had run her hand along Charlie's back when he was a foal, Pen who had handled his young feet and talked to him. Pen had helped walk Charlie when they first put a rope halter on him. Pen helped jog Charlie once in awhile, although she looked pretty scrawny for that to me. She was even making her ins with the new foal. One afternoon when I went out to the pasture to play with Sister Belle, there was Pen making over the foal.

And there was her relationship with Grandad. I saw how things stood the next morning after I met her.

First, Aunt Connie and I had gone over to the diner for breakfast without Grandad, as he'd said something about a ladder, and he'd get coffee in the tack room at the barn. I was glad to be alone with Aunt Connie, because I find it easier to make friends with people one at a time. I had decided I wasn't going to stay on the outside of that Hartshaw–Pen Greeley setup any longer than I had to. The afternoon before, Grandad had walked down in the pasture with me to show me Miss Maybelle and her foal, and we'd had a good low-key time together. So at breakfast I was concentrating on Aunt Connie, and we had a good time, too. I was beginning to see that basically she was a level-steady person—which was a good way to be around a spooky four-year-old like Scataway, probably—but she could loosen up and be fun. There were some guys in the café who were kidding with Aunt Connie, calling across the counter to her, and she was laughing and in a lot more talkative mood than usual. She told me how she'd bought Scataway at a sale when he was a two-year-old—"I just knew he was the colt for me!" And I told her how crazy I was about Charlie Stride. I shared that with her, and she liked it. She smiled and nodded at me, saying, "I know, I know." She didn't say anything then about Pen and Charlie, and I was grateful for that.

Then I took a big breath and asked, "Look, do you think I'll get to drive Charlie Stride today? I mean by myself on the cart. You know, just jog him around easy."

Aunt Connie forked up scrambled egg and shook her head as she chewed it. "I don't know," she said. "Charlie's got a lot of work to do today. Remember, he has his first race next week."

I hadn't really understood that before. Charlie

Stride, being a two-year-old, had never raced in competition. In a few days, at the early race at Athens, Iowa, Charlie would try out for the first time.

"Hey!" I said. "*Please,* can I go to Athens with you?"

She grinned. "Yeah, I guess you'd better."

Then she explained that the morning's work called for Charlie to have lessons in following a mobile starting gate. While we were eating, Grandad was tying a ladder crosswise to the back of the pickup truck, the idea being that a ladder looks something like a starting gate. A starting gate is a hinged metal framework of wings that is mounted on an automobile, and its purpose is to keep the horses in line and up to speed. As the horses follow the gate, they're moving thirty miles an hour by the time they cross the starting line. Then the gate wings fold up as the car speeds out of the way, off the track. As Aunt Connie explained the situation, I realized that a young colt who'd never had anything in front of his nose but the wind would need lessons in following a starting gate.

I said, "Huh, Charlie's still got a lot to learn, hasn't he?"

"He's just beginning," Aunt Connie said, picking up the check.

I was thinking, Good, I can learn with him.

So we got over to the track, and this is what I saw: Grandad was driving Charlie Stride behind the pickup, which had a ladder tied across its back end, and Pen was driving the pickup. Charlie Stride was snorting and dodging some, but Grandad was controlling him. Around the track they went, a happy threesome, working out together. That Pen! Only twelve years old, and already she could drive a truck.

I couldn't stand to watch. I followed Aunt Connie gloomily into the barn to help her hitch up Scataway, and I just stayed in there, moping around. Finally the yellow barn cat came along and smoothed against my leg, the only stroking I got that day.

Then Grandad and Pen came into the barn, and when they'd unhitched Charlie, lo and behold! Pen fed my grandfather strawberries! Well, she didn't exactly feed them to him, but she gave them to him. That sweet suck-up girl had gotten up way early and picked strawberries so Grandad would have something to eat with his coffee. I did notice that he didn't make a big scene over her bringing him strawberries, just ate them and said they were good.

But I got the picture. No wonder Grandad hadn't been aching and pining for his grandson to come for the summer. Pen was like a granddaughter to him, grandson and granddaughter rolled up in one. He called her "buddy," and they had a friendly easy relationship, working together with the horses. What did he need with a dumb city kid who didn't know anything about horses? I stood there watching him and her with those strawberries, and I felt as if he'd shoved me out the back door and locked it.

I didn't get to drive Charlie Stride that morning,

because later Grandad worked him for some fast miles, but the next day Grandad said to me,

"All right, buddy, let's see what you can do with Charlie Stride."

At last something good! I jumped to hitch the cart to Charlie's harness. The first time around the track I had to ride on Grandad's lap again, while he checked me out, but then he got off and gave me the reins.

"Remember, just take it easy," he said. "If he breaks stride, saw your reins to stop him and start over."

I nodded and started talking to the colt, "All right, Charlie, let's go."

I tried to touch him with the whip, the way Grandad did, but I was awkward, trying to hold both the reins and the whip. However, Charlie Stride had plenty of kid energy, and he wasn't about to stand around waiting. He moved off at a neat trot, speeding up a little when the lines were taut between us. I wasn't handy with the whip, but at least I kept a good grip on the reins. When he speeded up, I felt panicky for a second. What if all that powerful horse decided to take charge, and I couldn't control him? Charlie might be a colt, but he was as big as most horses. I hoped Pen wasn't watching. Still, I held the reins firmly, and Charlie didn't exceed the bit of speed he'd gotten up to.

Then, *click,* it was as if we'd settled in together, and the whole thing felt perfect. There was that smart colt, trotting along at a businesslike jog, his coat bright brown in the sunlight, and there I was, sitting right up behind his tail, driving him. The reins were taut and steady between us. I could feel him, and he could feel me. As we spun along, around the track, I heard a meadowlark call, heard Charlie's hooves, *clop-clop,* breathed the dust and hay smell, and it came to me that I was perfectly happy. There was no place in the world that I'd rather be, nothing in the world that I'd rather be doing. Now that's happiness!

As the colt came out of a turn, he speeded up a little, and it seemed to me that his trot faltered, so I slacked and sawed the reins just a little. And he didn't break gait, but trotted on as neatly as ever, *clop-clop.* Just for that first time of driving Charlie alone, it was given to me that I couldn't do anything wrong, as if that one time was meant to be perfect.

Even Grandad was grinning at me when we wheeled off the track, at last. I wonder what my face looked like, that he grinned so.

Charlie acted as if he'd enjoyed the trip as much as I had. As I led him back into the barn, talking to him all the way, he kept butting my shoulder with his nose and kind of skipping his feet. Then I saw Pen. She was over by a stall gate, watching me and the brown horse. She was just standing there, chewing on one of her tails of hair and watching us. She didn't say anything. Neither did I. I went ahead with wiping down Charlie until she went away.

Well, I'm glad I had that one perfect time with Charlie Stride, because as the days went by, I felt more and more sour about Pen. She was just always there, and Grandad "buddied" her a lot more than he did me.

I don't think the Hartshaws noticed how I reacted to Pen. They seemed to assume that Pen and I would be friends. Of course, I didn't give up on Grandad. I tried not to make any big goof-ups with the horses, tried to learn fast about everything at the barn, and I tried to be extra friendly with Grandad at night, when we were back at the farm. But by then he was tired and didn't want to talk. Actually, he never did want to talk about anything but horses.

Of course, I wasn't bored with the horses—I could never be bored with Charlie Stride—but it was a pretty steady dose of the same thing, and I wished we could do something else once in awhile. Like maybe see something of Iowa. Instead, every morning we went to the barn and took care of the horses, worked them out and gave them their noon feed. Every afternoon one of us would check Miss Maybelle and Sister Belle in the pasture and feed them. Every evening we went back to the barn to give the horses their last feed and maybe walk them a little. There were no days off, although on Sunday the Hartshaws didn't work the horses.

After all my trying, it was the thing about the circus that really made me mad, even though it was a little thing. I found out there was going to be a circus on Saturday over in Trumbell, where Grandad had picked me up from the train. I had never seen a circus, and I got fired up to go. But when I asked Grandad about it, he said,

"Sorry, can't take the time from the horses."

I said, "But look, I've never seen a circus, and we could have a neat time."

"Sorry." He shook his head.

I said, "OK, I'll go by myself!"

"Suit yourself," he told me.

I was red-hot mad. Grandad hadn't made any effort to show me around, let a city kid see some of the country sights. And as a matter of fact, he and Aunt Connie never did all summer. I didn't get to any of the town celebrations unless there was a horse race connected to the local events. The Hartshaws same as said, We've got no spare time for you, kid; come along with our way of life, if you want to.

Well, I got myself to the circus via the bus and used up nearly all the money I'd brought to Iowa, since Grandad didn't offer me any. But be-darn! I was determined I'd enjoy the circus, just to spite him. And I did like it pretty well, although I kept thinking through the lion act and the high-wire performances that I'd have enjoyed it more if Grandad had come along like a real grandfather.

But no, he couldn't leave his precious horses, even for one afternoon. However, I found out he would trust a neighbor to check the mare and foal in the pasture, while we were gone overnight to Athens.

"Couldn't Pen do it?" I asked when I heard that.

Aunt Connie said, "Why, she's going with us."

It was as if she'd punched me. The idea of Pen going with us to the races had never occurred to me. But it figured: it was Charlie Stride's first race, and since Pen had helped train him, maybe it was natural she'd want to see how he performed his first time out. And after that—

"Geez, she's not going with us to *all* the races, is she?" I begged.

"What's the matter, don't you like Pen?" Aunt Connie said. "The way you're so friendly, I thought you'd have made friends with a kid your age by now."

"Ah, she's all right," I mumbled, and Aunt Connie let it go at that.

I turned to making friends with Boyd Gray. After all, I'd come to Iowa to be with a man, not a barnful of women. And Boyd was a friendly guy, maybe not a big talker, but at least he didn't act like he had to pay a dollar for every word he said. He told me about some of his racing experiences and answered my questions and even asked me a few about Colorado. Even though Boyd had a good horse, he wasn't competitive about the Hartshaw horses. One day we were standing together by the fence, watching, when Charlie broke stride. Grandad was taking him for a fast brush, when next thing the colt was tossing his head and trying to gallop, and Grandad was sawing away at the reins, trying to pull him up.

"Why does he keep doing that?" I almost wailed. "He keeps breaking!"

Boyd said, "Ah, don't worry. Colts do that. He'll learn."

But he frowned a little, rubbing his cheek, and later when Grandad came off the track Boyd told him he'd observed how Charlie was swinging his legs and suggested something about a horseshoe of a different weight. Grandad agreed and had Charlie reshod that afternoon.

The next day we all had something to be happy about, because Charlie Stride trotted the mile around the Olden track in 2:14, and he didn't break! Granddad clocked him with a watch in his hand as he drove, and Aunt Connie stood at the fence rail with another stopwatch. Two-fourteen for a maiden colt! The top trotting record is about 1:55, less than twenty seconds faster. Wow, were we happy and excited! Charlie Stride, too. As he trotted off the track, he fairly danced, throwing his head up as if he could hardly wait to race again. I kept praying, Let Charlie Stride not break in the race and not lame himself, either, when he gets out there with the other colts at Athens.

The early races at Athens, my first glorious race day—I still feel bad when I think how I messed up that day. All I saw of Athens was the track at the Saddle Club, and that was enough. I'd just as soon never see Athens, Iowa, again, although I suppose I will next summer. At least I won't make the same mistake I did at Charlie Stride's first race.

Of course, at the beginning I was in hog heaven with all the horses and excitement. When we got there, it was like a carnival getting set up—lots of men and their horses and wives, everybody milling around and calling out happy greetings and leading horses into stalls in the barns. "How-da!" Aunt Connie kept calling to friends, "How you been?" Grandad was carefully backing Charlie Stride out of the trailer, and when Charlie hit real earth again, he cut up worse than I'd ever seen him, jumping around like he was going to tear right back to Olden.

"Hey, Hartshaw, forget to cut the frogs out of his feet?" a man said. "That the new colt?"

Grandad smiled and said, "Yessir. Look out for Charlie Stride!"

We'd driven down to Athens in two pickup trucks, hauling the horses in their trailers. I rode with Aunt Connie, and Pen rode with Grandad. Scataway wouldn't ride in a trailer with another horse, so Aunt Connie pulled him, and Grandad hauled the other two horses. We went the day before the race, so the horses could rest in the barns overnight.

Miss Loubelle D. came out of her trailer and went into her stall as neatly as if she'd been doing it all her life, which I guess she had. But Charlie Stride acted just plain mad and insulted at that kind of treatment, being whisked through the countryside and then put into a strange stall with a lot of new smells. He fought and pulled when Grandad was leading him into the barn, and as soon as he got into his stall, he began kicking it. Both Charlie Stride and Scataway are geldings, and a good thing, because those two horses acted feisty enough, even gelded. I was helping unload the sulkies, but I could hear Charlie kicking and neighing in the barn. Poor Charlie, I thought. I headed into the barn to talk to him and see if I could calm him down. So what did I see when I got there? Pen. *She* was standing at his stall gate, sweet-talking him, and he did calm down for her, too. Shoot! I wheeled out of there before she saw me.

At last we could eat and go to bed. Aunt Connie and Pen had a room at a motel nearby, but Grandad and I slept on blankets out behind the barns.

Grandad always wanted to spend the night near the stalls, to make sure no one bothered the horses. Not all the drivers did that. Some who lived near brought their horses in the day of the race, some brought along little house trailers and parked them near the horse barns, and some stayed in the motels.

Tired as I was, I didn't sleep much that night. After we ate, Grandad and I sat in the barn talking with some other guys until well after dark, which came late, because it was near Midsummer Day. I really liked that, just us men in the barn, sitting around on the trunks full of horse supplies, no puny girls butting in. Then when we stretched out on our blankets in the grass behind the barn, I couldn't go to sleep because I was so happy. I lay there with a big old maple tree rustling over me in a bit of night breeze and the stars shining above the tree, remembering some of the talk about horses and hearing the peaceful summer night sounds of crickets and an occasional stomp or whuffle from the horses in the barn. I thought, Here I am, just ten days away from Denver, lying in the grass behind a horse barn in Iowa, with a race tomorrow. No city streets, no traffic noises and sirens, no apartment, just horses and stars and a countryside that smells even greener at night than it does in the daytime. After I'd finally dozed off, I thought I heard Charlie's whinny, and I went in the barn to see if he was all right. He was only standing there asleep, leaning up against a back corner of the stall. Tired brown horse, gathering up his strength for tomorrow, I thought. I stood there smiling at him for a little while, then I went back to my blanket and finally got to sleep.

Morning happened shortly after that, with the sun rising and shining in my eyes at about 4 A.M. I turned over and went back to sleep for awhile, but gradually I heard more and more sounds from the barns, and then I smelled coffee. Grandad's blanket was empty. Going into the barn, I found Grandad and a few other men standing around drinking coffee.

Grandad greeted me like one of the bunch. "Morning, buddy, want some coffee?"

"Sure," I said and drank my first cup of coffee. It was so hot and strong I choked, but it was a great feeling to be there with the men on the morning of a race—and no Pen around.

What with getting up so early, and the races not happening until 1 P.M., that morning seemed to stretch out for a full day. By noon it was all a blur of watching horses jog around the track, helping with the chores, and talking with all kinds of people, as we stood watching at the fence rail. I remember seeing a horse trotting with a tin can tied under his chin and somebody telling me the can was to make the horse keep his head up. I remember seeing an old gentleman taking a pacer around the track and a man beside me telling that Mr. Smith was eighty-six years old and still jogging horses for his son.

"You're never too old for this sport," the man said. "That's another thing I like about it!"

And I particularly remember seeing Jake Bottle. Aunt Connie was leaning against the fence next to me then, and she pointed to a driver coming around the turn with a dark bay mare. He was whipping her.

"Watch her break," Aunt Connie said.

The mare did, right after she headed into the homestretch. The man pulled her to a stop, then jerked her around and drove off the track toward us.

"Come on," Aunt Connie said. "Let's save that mare from one beating, anyway."

The man who jumped out of the sulky looked fierce enough to eat a snake, and he yanked the poles loose from the horse's harness without speaking to anyone. He had deep lines in his face, a sharp nose, and red hair just a little darker than mine, which is red gold. I shivered suddenly. A man with red hair nearly like mine, who beats horses . . . no wonder. . . . Jake Bottle led the horse into the barn, hurrying, and we followed him. As he shoved the mare into a stall, Aunt Connie spoke up.

"Howdy, Jake. Looked like Rocket Queen was making good speed today."

At Aunt Connie's voice he jerked around, and I almost grinned. If he'd been about to slap the mare, he couldn't do it now, with us there. Or would he?

He smacked the flat of his hand down on Rocket Queen's back, as if it was an affectionate smack, but it was a little too hard.

"She'll do all right," he said briefly, turning, as if he expected us to go away.

We didn't, though. Aunt Connie stayed around, making talk, and then moved down to our stalls, but still near. No beating or cursing happened in Rocket Queen's stall, and Aunt Connie winked at me as she brushed Scataway.

"Will he race against Charlie Stride?" I whispered.

Yes, she told me in a low voice, Jake Bottle had a young colt that would race with Charlie Stride in the maiden class—horses and mares that had never had a win. Rocket Queen would race in the same heats with Scataway.

Four races were scheduled for that afternoon, each of them to be run in two heats. That meant that actually each group of horses would race twice, and the winners of each heat would earn part of the money purse put up for the race. The first race was for the fairly young pacers, which included Scataway and that mare of Jake Bottle's. The second race, Charlie Stride's race, was for two-year-old trotters making their first start; after that the maiden pacers would race, and last there was a pacing event for the older and presumably faster horses. Miss Loubelle D. would race in that one, "driven by George Hartshaw," it said on the program.

I could feel the tension building up as we got close to starting time. Although this wasn't a county fair, lots of people kept arriving for the races, some of them coming to the barns, but most of them climbing up in the grandstand to get a good seat, calling back and forth, a happy crowd. The drivers and horses were having their final warm-up trips around the track, and some of them were getting nervous. A piece of harness broke on one horse, and there was some frantic running around, getting it replaced. One driver, warming up, came whooshing around the track, yelling, "Heeyuh!" and whipping his horse in a brush. When Grandad came around with Charlie, however, I heard him whistling and saying, "Yes sir," gently as ever.

But even Aunt Connie was keyed up. When she was putting the racing harness on Scataway, I saw her fastening a kind of eye shield on his head and asked her what that was.

"A blinder bridle," she snapped. "Stand out of the way!"

Scataway jumped a little, and Aunt Connie cheeked his bridle, saying, "Ho, man!"

Then she must have realized she was getting too tense, because she kind of smoothed herself down and talked about Scataway as she worked on him.

"Never saw such a skittish three-year-old as he was last year," she said. "He'd shy if a butterfly sailed by. Or, racing, he'd watch cigarette smoke curling up until I thought he was going to take me into the fence. I put everything I could think of on Scataway's head— a shadow roll, a peekaboo bridle. Finally I put a blinder bridle on him, and now he can't see anything but straight ahead."

"Why did you fool with all that, if he's so much trouble?" I asked.

"Why, because he's a great racer!" Aunt Connie patted his haunch. "You watch!"

I did, and it was a great race. I stood at the fence rail along with the other horse people from the barns, and I was so excited I didn't even care that Pen was standing alongside me. First, the announcer up in the judges' stand opposite the grandstand, called for the drivers to parade their horses, and they all took a fancy little sprint down the track. Aunt Connie and Scataway looked royal, the handsome dark horse flashing in the sunlight and Aunt Connie sitting up proudly behind, wearing the Hartshaw racing silks, maroon and silver on white. Then all the horses came out of the backstretch and lined up behind the starting gate. They came along right in front of me, where I was standing by the fence on the curve before the homestretch.

In the drawing, Jake Bottle and Rocket Queen had drawn the pole position, the best of all, number one on the inside rail, which had fussed Aunt Connie a little, because she'd drawn the number three spot. However, as soon as the horses passed the starting line, the number two horse pulled into the lead, with Rocket Queen following on the rail. Scataway raced alongside Rocket Queen. I didn't see what happened in the shuffling for position on the first turn, the other side of the track from me, but when the horses came into the backstretch, Scataway was still racing on the outside of Rocket Queen. He looked beautiful, swaying from side to side in the pace, streamlining himself around the turn, with Aunt Connie urging him on.

I jumped and yelled, "Come on, Scataway!" and I became aware that Pen was yelling, too, leaning out over the fence. She did have vocal cords like a real person, after all. But even her yelling couldn't help Scataway win.

The Athens track was a half-mile track, so the horses went around again to make the mile. Aunt Connie raced next to Bottle past the grandstand, but when I could see the field in the backstretch again, Scataway had fallen back, and the number four horse was pulling ahead of Rocket Queen. Jake Bottle's face was awful. As the horses pounded past us, Bottle's mouth was a big bellows hole, and he was whipping Rocket Queen. Right past me she broke stride, and he had to pull her to the outside, and that was all of the race for Rocket Queen. The number four horse won, and Scataway came in third.

All the horses jogged slowly back past the grandstand as the announcer said to each driver, "Thank you, Mr. Baker," "Thank you, Miss Hartshaw," and each driver tipped his whip, all very polite. But when Aunt Connie got back to the barn, she was madder than heck.

"That Bottle kept me parked out so long, Scataway just used himself up. That—"

She snapped her mouth shut and set to sponging the lather off her horse. I asked what "parked out" meant, and she said, "Kept me on the outside. Scataway had to cover more ground than the horses next

68

to the inside rail."

I brought the bucket of water for Scataway, while she got a blanket on him. Scataway was really blowing, but he still threw his legs around, as if the race had made him mad, too. I offered the bucket to Scataway, and Aunt Connie called impatiently,

"Hold it higher. Don't make him bend his neck down when he's hot. He could cramp his windpipe."

She was being awfully particular, I thought, because I hadn't heard of anything like that at Olden.

After Scataway drank, Aunt Connie walked him behind the barn, and they both calmed down, the horse flicking his ears as Connie talked to him, her voice quiet then. From a stall near the back of the barn I heard smacking sounds, a whinny and some swear words. Poor Rocket Queen.

However, it only lasted for a few seconds, because it was time for the next race. Bottle was taking out his colt, and I realized Grandad and Pen had already led Charlie Stride out of the barn. Charlie's big moment! His first race! I didn't want to miss one inch of that, and I started to run around the barn toward the track. Aunt Connie called me back.

"Scataway is cooled out pretty good. Put him in his stall and give him another sip of water in a few minutes," she said. "I've got to see this race!"

And *she* hurried off to see Charlie Stride perform for the first time.

They were all out there, concentrating on Charlie —Grandad, Aunt Connie and Pen—while I was left

back in the barn with Scataway. Nobody recognized that I might have some special interest in Charlie Stride's first race, nobody thought of him as *my* sweet buddy. I was just low man on the stack, doing groom's work in the barn. As I led Scataway into his stall, I heard the announcer saying, "Parade your horses, gentlemen," and I just had to get out there. Surely, I thought, Aunt Connie hadn't meant for me to stay with her horse throughout the whole race. I

held the bucket up for Scataway to take another
drink, and then I dashed out of the barn to the fence
rail.

Charlie Stride's first race was a beautiful beginning for that great colt. He couldn't do anything
wrong. He started in the number two position, but
at the first turn Grandad maneuvered him next to
the inside rail and ahead of the lead horse, and that
really was the horse race. Because Charlie Stride just

stayed the front-runner all the rest of the way. What a horse to watch! His body was brown power streaking along, legs flashing in perfect stride, never breaking the trot, *my* horse, leading the pack!

"Come on, Charlie Stride!" I was yelling. "Wow! Oh, wow, Charlie!"

Down the fence rail I heard Pen screaming, too, "Charlie, Charlie, Charlie darling!" *Darling,* ugh!

Grandad looked steady as a rock, sitting there on his sulky, leading that field of skittish young colts. Hardly the activity you'd expect of a stolid haystack, yet Grandad looked perfectly right out there, as he held the reins and leaned to flick his whip. The second time around, Jake Bottle and his dumb colt were falling back, but one of the other horses tried to pull ahead of Charlie Stride on the turn in front of me. I saw Grandad touch Charlie's black tail with the whip, and Charlie let out more speed. That brown horse just leaned forward and sailed right on down the homestretch for the finish wire.

"WOW!" I screamed. "We won! Charlie Stride! Charlie Stride!"

The crowd was shouting, too, especially when the judges announced Charlie Stride's time: 2:12.3. He'd trotted the mile in two minutes, twelve and three-fifths seconds. That was a great record for a colt on his maiden try. Then the drivers were parading their horses back past the grandstand, with the annnouncer saying, "Thank you, Mr. Bottle, thank you, Mr. Jones," and finally, for the winner, "Thank you, Mr. Hartshaw!"

And then Aunt Connie broke on me like a thunderstorm in July.

"Randy Meister!" she yelled, grabbing me away from the fence. "Are you crazy? Why did you leave that bucket of water with Scataway?"

The horses and sulkies were coming off the track into the area in front of the barns. Aunt Connie jerked me into our barn and down the passage, yelling all the way.

"You may have foundered him! I still don't know —you—" She shook me, dragging me along.

We ended in front of Scataway's stall. The bucket of water was sitting outside the stall gate, and there was still some water in it.

"How much did he drink?" she demanded.

I stared at my furious aunt. Her face was puckered up with rage. "I don't understand," I stammered, "I don't—don't know what you're talking about."

"The water!" she spit out. "If a hot horse drinks too much water, he'll founder. And you—you—you left the bucket in his stall, where he could drink all he wanted! Bending his neck down, too!"

I looked at the bucket and couldn't even remember leaving it in the stall. In the past week I'd learned you had to water a hot horse slowly, but I hadn't paid any attention to the "why" of it. For me, the important part about watering Charlie Stride was the chance to be with him.

Looking at the bit of water in the bottom of the

bucket, I tried to remember how much there'd been when I gave Scataway his last drink, but I couldn't.

"Aunt Connie," I pleaded, "I didn't fill the bucket very full in the first place. He couldn't have drunk very much. Look, he's all right, isn't he?"

Scataway was just standing in his stall watching us and twitching his ears. In the stall next to him, Miss Loubelle D. blew gently out of her nose.

"No, I don't know he's all right!" Aunt Connie cried. "I don't dare race him in the next heat. And if he—oh, Lord, Scataway may never run again! All because you—you half-brained—can't trust you to do even the —"

She was looking at me and talking to me as if I was scum. This woman, knowing it all, overreacting, hollering at me—all of a sudden I hated her.

"Listen!" I yelled. "I wanted to see Charlie Stride race, too! Is that such a crime? Leaving me back here in the barn—"

"If you had the sense God gave a goose," she began in a low tight voice—maybe because people and horses were coming into the barn.

"Sense!" I said. "You oughtta get some sense about people! All you ever think about is the horse, the horse always comes first. What about me? What about my feelings?"

She was staring at me. Other people were looking at me, and I saw Grandad leading Charlie Stride into the barn. I turned and ran out the back end of the barn, because, damn it, I was going to cry again.

4

ON THE DRIVE BACK TO OLDEN I RODE WITH GRAN-
dad, and neither of us had anything to say for a long
time. I'd stayed away from the Hartshaws for the rest
of the afternoon, but it was as if I'd jinxed the day.
Nothing really went right for the Hartshaw horses in
the rest of the races. Miss Loubelle D. came in second
and third in her heats, and Charlie Stride broke gait
in his second heat. "Charlie Stride making a little
riffle," the announcer said. I was standing by myself
at the fence, and I just couldn't believe it when I saw
him joggling around in the backstretch. That was the
last misery of the afternoon.

Even before that I was miserable enough, because
when I got done feeling sorry for myself, I began to
worry about Scataway. If he was foundered and
never could race again—oh, geez, what a terrible
thing. Terrible both for the horse and for Aunt Connie, because it was obvious that her whole life was

tied up in that horse. I tried to remember how much water I'd run into the bucket in the first place, hoping I'd been lazy and not filled it up. I didn't know then what foundering meant, or what it would do to a horse, but it sounded very final. It sounded like a sinking ship.

Then, during the heat in which Scataway should have run, but didn't, Pen came over to me. I didn't know she was at my elbow until she leaned forward on the fence.

She said, "Grandad says—" *Grandad,* she called him!—"says Scataway will probably be all right. Connie has been watching his feet, but they don't seem to be getting tender, so he probably didn't founder himself on the water. He doesn't show any signs of colic, so far, either. Don't feel so bad."

I felt a rocket of relief, and I let out a big breath. "Wow!" I said to Pen, but then I saw her freckled face looking at me, and I felt clouded over again. I didn't want any comforting from her.

"Huh!" I said and moved up the fence rail, away from her.

So it was a rotten day at Athens, Iowa. Riding back in the pickup, I kept catching myself chewing my fingernails. I didn't know what to think, or where I went from there with the Hartshaws, or whether I even wanted to.

It was Grandad who finally broke the silence. Out of nowhere, he said, "Charles Williams. Now there was a man who loved horses, Charles Williams."

It startled me that he's actually volunteered a statement. So far I'd found him so close with conversation that most of the time I had to pry things out of him. Like, I'd ask, "Did Miss Loubelle D. ever have any especially exciting races?" "Yep," he'd say. I'd wait and finally ask, "Well, what were they?" And he'd say, "Oh, the one at Bottville, the one at Sedalia." Geez!

But there in the pickup he began talking about Charles Williams, an old-time Iowa horse trainer and driver, how great Williams was with horses and how he put his theories to work in handling horses.

"It all boiled down to this," Grandad said. "Charles Williams said, 'Always think he will *surely* prove to be a great colt if you develop him as you should. Keep thinking *the least inattention on your part* would make your horse worthless'."

He stopped, was silent again. He'd spoken those words as if he were quoting God.

Yes, I thought, that's great—a great dig at me. True, too, probably, if all you cared about was horses. But I wasn't the kind of complete horse nut that Grandad and Aunt Connie were. Sure, naturally, I'd do anything for Charlie Stride—I thought of him riding behind us in the trailer and hoped he was all right. Yet that was a case of *one* horse, and I could see by then that when the Hartshaws said, "The horse comes first," they meant *any* horse, all horses.

I was still mad. Ashamed, too, probably. I

thought, They're all one way about horses, Grandad and Aunt Connie, and what's more, they're shallow. They're shallow because all they think about is The Horse. They don't know or care anything about what's going on in the world, or people, or human relationships. Just horses. Grandad didn't even notice how Pen worshiped him, let alone my efforts to be friends.

I got to thinking about this thing of who comes first. I simply couldn't figure how a grandfather could think more of his horse than he did of his grandson. The thing is—I can see it now—I'd always been pretty self-centered. Maybe every kid is. Why not? I live inside myself. I know more about me— how I feel, what makes me hurt, what makes me happy—than I know about anyone else. So why shouldn't I come first with me? But then I got all tangled up in my thinking as I rode along beside Grandad. He seemed to be telling me I should always think of the horse before myself. He was telling me how to shape up, according to his standards. But I wanted *him* to shape up. A real grandfather would have seen how bad I felt over the mistake I'd made with Scataway—he saw me crying behind the barn, I know—how bad I felt over all the mistakes I'd made. Not that Grandad had yelled at me, the way Aunt Connie did; but when we were loading the trucks, I tried to tell him I was sorry about Scataway, and he only shook his head, saying, " 'Sorry' doesn't mend." A real grandfather would have seen how all along I'd tried to make friends with him and responded a little. Like, he could have forgiven me. That's what I thought.

So we rode through the Iowa countryside, and it got dark, and the two of us were shut up together in the cab of the truck, going through the dark. I hadn't said anything yet on the trip. All of a sudden I thought, I'll try him one more time, just to see if he'll open up on something besides horses.

I said, "I miss Grandma. Do you?" I asked questions: "Were you born in Iowa?" "What did you want to be when you grew up?" "What's winter like in Iowa?"

Nothing. He just grunted short answers. I couldn't get him started on anything. Not only did I have a grandfather who was never going to like me, but he was a man who just wasn't there on anything but horses.

At that point I really would have gone back to Denver the next morning, if it hadn't been for Charlie Stride. Riding along in the truck I got to thinking about him, how he'd looked racing around the track, his long legs reaching out in the trot, and then seeing him again as he broke stride and pulled up. I'd only known Charlie for eleven days, yet already that long-legged bundle of high-spirited horse had such a pull on me that it would be like going away and leaving part of myself in Olden. I could hear his friendly whinny as I came near his stall, see his ears perking toward me, feel his nose butting my chest. I remembered the feel of him through the reins when I drove him.

"Why did Charlie Stride break gait?" I asked Grandad.

"Well, it happens," he said. "First race and all, maybe he was nervous. But I'm kinda worried about him, way he keeps breaking stride. Not dependable. Like today, he was going along steady, then I felt him kind of ripple, and he jumped off stride." He mused on that awhile, then said, as if reassuring himself, "Maybe he felt he could go faster, and I was holding him back too much."

Grandad said he hadn't wanted to call on Charlie Stride for his top speed his first race, but that colt surely did want to go fast.

"Right from the first he was a horse that would take hold of you, running. If I can just let Charlie take me at his speed, bring him along within himself," Grandad said, "I think we got us a winner in that boy!" He'd started speaking softly, as if talking to himself, but his voice rang out like "victory!" on the last words.

"Yeah!" I said happily.

I went into a daydream, seeing Charlie Stride winning a race, nosing ahead past the wire, legs flashing. I pictured me driving Charlie fast around a track, his black tail flaring out over my knees. I could just feel us working together, a team racing to the finish wire. Suddenly, the thing I wanted more than anything in the world was to drive Charlie Stride fast.

I wanted to feel us racing around a track, both of us in control of our share and signaling back and forth through the reins. I pictured me pulling the left rein, signaling, "Quick, duck in next to the rail on this turn," or holding the lines firmly, telling, "Save yourself, Charlie, for the big effort later." And the feeling of Charlie's power surging through the reins, saying, "I'm strong and steady," or "I've got lots more speed to let out, let's go!"

I knew I had worlds to learn before I could drive Charlie Stride in a race. First, I just wanted to find out how it would feel to drive him fast, one brush at top speed. By the time we got back to Olden that night, I had decided to watch for my chance.

When we unloaded the horses at the barn, I apologized to Aunt Connie. I had a stiff time doing it, but I knew I had to if I was going to stay in Olden. I wasn't sorry for telling her she didn't care about people's feelings, but I was really sorry I'd threatened Scataway, and I told her so.

She only gave me a tired look and said, "OK, Randy."

She was leading Scataway into his stall. I studied his slim legs, and they looked all right to me.

"What would happen if he's foundered?" I made myself ask.

His feet would get inflamed, she told me. The tissue would be damaged. Eventually his legs might get bowed, and his hooves start to peel. And, "No foot, no horse," she said.

So there it was, how close I'd come to making "no horse" out of Scataway. I saw Aunt Connie's hand tremble on the stall gate as she closed it, and on impulse I reached out, put my hand over hers. Looking her in the eye I told her what I really felt.

"I'm sorry about Scataway," I said. "I really mean it."

When I went to bed that night, though, all I could think about was Charlie Stride and driving him fast. For awhile I thought my chance would never come. The next day Grandad said we'd only walk the horses, to give them a rest after the races, so we didn't hitch them up to the carts. Aunt Connie was watching Scataway closely, but he wasn't foundered, she was sure. Pen didn't show up at the track that day— later I heard that her mother had snagged her to do some work at home, to make up for being gone to Athens—so I had Charlie Stride all to myself. I had a fine time currying him and telling him what a great colt he was, while he pricked his ears at my voice and nickered back that I wasn't a bad sort, myself. Charlie Stride certainly had more sparkle to him than anybody I met last summer. Later I led him over to where Grandad was walking Miss Loubelle D.

"Do you think I could drive Charlie Stride fast sometime?" I asked, as casually as I could.

"No," he said and walked the mare away from me.

Well, I wasn't going to push it anymore, trying to be friends with Grandad, but at least he could be a source of information about horses. I followed him and asked a few questions about speeding with a horse and found out one thing: that you never make a colt go hard for a full mile, but only for a quarter or an eighth of a mile. Otherwise, he might get "bad-headed," as Grandad put it, thinking he had to go hard every time he hit the track.

I had decided I was going to have my fast trip with Charlie no matter what Grandad said. However, I was a little worried about what might happen if Charlie got to going too fast and I couldn't stop him. So I asked,

"How do you get a horse to slow down, when he's going hard?"

Grandad said, "Oh, it's conditioning. I always use the same words and tone of voice, 'All right, easy,' and then I slack the reins a little, the way I showed you, or saw the reins. The horse gets to know."

OK, I thought, so I'm ready.

But then the day after that I didn't get a chance, either, because Charlie Stride showed a side of him that so far I'd only heard about. He acted headstrong, just plain determined to have his own way. He fought a little when Grandad harnessed him, and then when Grandad tried to drive him out to the track, he reared up. My nice brown horse stood up on his hind legs and climbed the air, whinnying and snorting, almost tilted Grandad out of the cart. Grandad went to his head and pulled him down, talking soothingly to Charlie, and then he tried to drive him again. The colt went into the same kind of fit, rearing and struggling in the harness.

"What's the matter with him?" I asked Aunt Connie, who was standing by me, watching.

"Guess he doesn't want to work," she said. "Maybe he's all upset from the excitement of going to his first race."

As a yearling, Charlie Stride had "rared" a lot, she said, until they wondered if they'd ever make a racehorse of him. Then they'd brought in a man who specialized in breaking horses, and he'd gotten Charlie Stride settled down after a session with a W-line. That was a rope tied to the horse's front legs, making a "W" to the back legs, Aunt Connie explained. When the horse reared, the W-line pulled his front legs out from under him, and he'd go down on his nose.

"Sounds kind of cruel, but it isn't," Aunt Connie said. "After three or four times on his nose, Charlie Stride learned to 'whoa' when we said 'whoa'."

However, the brown colt seemed to have forgotten his lesson, because Grandad couldn't get him to behave. He went in the tack room to call the trainer, to see if he could come over right away with his W-line.

"Never let a horse get away with doing something wrong," Aunt Connie said.

So the rest of that morning was spent in getting Charlie Stride gentled down. I felt sorry for him, because despite what Aunt Connie said, it looked cruel to me. After the first time I saw poor Charlie come

crashing down on his nose I couldn't watch. They
had all that rope tied around his legs, and he tried to
rear, and he came down on his knees, *bang*. I cried
out, "Oh, no! He'll break a leg!" Aunt Connie gave
me a dirty look. She said, "He won't make much of a
racehorse if he can't take falling a few times." So I
moped off into the barn and stayed there. Maybe
Charlie couldn't go rearing and fighting just whenever he felt like it, yet I thought it seemed such a
show of human power, bringing a horse to his knees.

Naturally, I didn't dare try to sneak Charlie
Stride out for a fast run that day, after all the trouble
he'd been through. But the idea kept burning at me.
I felt as if things wouldn't be settled down and right
until Charlie and I had the thrill of working together
on a fast run.

That afternoon at the farm the Hartshaws disap-
peared, as usual, Grandad to take a nap and Aunt
Connie to fill out forms in the little office off the living room, but I was too keyed up to settle anywhere.
Besides, it was too sweltering hot in the house to rest.
I wandered out through the deserted barnyard,
looked at the motionless stands of cornstalks beyond
the fence, and then headed down the pasture to look
for Miss Maybelle and the foal. Miss Maybelle was
an awfully nice motherly horse, a very dark bay like
Scataway. She'd started as a pacer in the races, but
she'd broken a bone in her leg when she was a three-
year-old—"Put her foot right through a bike wheel
that came too close," Aunt Connie had said—so

Grandad had made a brood mare of her. She was Charlie Stride's mother, and that made me especially fond of her. I thought I'd tell her how ornery her son had acted that morning, but then I saw her and the foal dozing in the shade of some big oak trees, and I decided not to bother them. They looked so peaceful, the mother standing with her head drooping over the foal, who was lying on the ground, all long legs jacked up. My clothes were sticking to me in the heat, and I thought of the creek and how good it would feel to get in the water. Yeah, I thought, I'll go swimming.

The creek wasn't deep enough for swimming, but there was one place where it made a pretty good pool at the base of a low limestone cliff shoving out of the hill. I followed the horse path down through the woods to the stream, and I was glad I'd had the idea, because it was a good place to be on a hot afternoon. It was cooler under the big trees down there, with the water rippling over brown rocks and sandy places. Only a few bits of sunlight got through the trees to flicker on the water. I waded down the creek toward the pool—the water cool on my feet through my sneakers. I could hardly wait to get my clothes off. Then I saw Pen.

I came around the rocky shoulder, and there she was, sitting on a big boulder, her feet in the water. She had a fishing pole with a line hanging in the pool where I planned to swim. She saw me and said, "Hi." No expression on her face, whether she was surprised, glad, or sorry to see me, just "Hi."

"Huh," I said. "I was going to swim here."

"Well, I'm fishing here," she said.

She went on holding the pole with the line in the water. Even I could tell that wasn't much of a way to fish.

"Ever catch anything?" I asked.

She said, "Sure."

"Ah, come on," I said, "you're not really fishing. Nobody catches fish in the middle of a hot day. Fish don't bite then."

Pen didn't say anything, just looked at the water. I itched with sweat, and the pool looked so cool.

"Look, I'm going to swim here," I told her. "You come back later when the fish—if there are any—are biting. I bet your mother wants you, little girl."

She looked at me, her lips tightening. "I was here first," she said.

"Good for you. And I'm here next," I said, peeling off my shirt.

When I started to unfasten my pants, Pen jumped up on her rock.

"What are you doing!" she exclaimed.

"Taking off my clothes, dumbbell," I said, grinning. "Told you I was going to swim here."

Instead of looking mad and yelling at me, Pen just cocked her head, staring at me, then pulled her line out of the water and ran away. She just gave in, no spirit at all. She'd be no fun to fight with, I thought.

My chance with Charlie Stride came a few days

later. One night at supper Grandad announced that it was time for him and Aunt Connie to harvest the oats—"good oats make good horses." They'd be tied up with harvesting for the next two days, he said, and Pen and I were to do the chores for the horses.

"Just slow-jog them once each morning," he told me. "Pen will be there to help."

He looked at me across the table in a speculating way, and I expected Grandad to add something like, Do what Pen tells you, or, Take good care of my horses, or even, For the Lord's sake, stay out of trouble. But he just nodded once at me and went back to digging mashed potatoes off his plate.

Aunt Connie did add something, though. She said, "Let Pen jog Scataway."

Simply an order, no smile with her statement. I could see it was going to be a long time before Aunt Connie trusted me.

"For sure," I said as lightly as I could.

I wished I could have the horses all to myself, no Pen anywhere in sight, but of course the Hartshaws wouldn't trust me alone with the horses without big neat experienced Pen along. The green beans tasted bitter in my mouth. Still, Grandad must have some faith in my driving ability, I realized, or he wouldn't let me jog the horses at all. Just that morning he'd let me drive Charlie Stride again, watching from the fence rail with no comment. I must have done all right. I was glad I hadn't given in to the urge to speed Charlie up and give him a whirl.

After supper Grandad hauled an old bicycle out of the barn, said I could ride it back and forth to the fairground. I spent the evening patching the front tire and pumping it up with a hand pump, and the next morning I rode off to town on it. The Hartshaws set off at the same time, heading down the road the other direction for their oat field. For the operation, Grandad was going to drive the combine, and Aunt Connie would drive the truck the oats were loaded onto. I had to admit, they were quite a team.

The bicycle was a heavy wobbly old thing, but I felt good as I rode along between the fields. The dew still shone fresh on the grass, and so many birds were singing in the early morning that it sounded as if the air should be thick with birds. That's one thing I especially remember about the summer in Olden, lots of bird song early every morning. I never hear birds in Denver, because for one thing, I'm not up that early, and for another thing, I haven't seen many birds around our apartment house. As I cycled along I sang with the birds, "Charlie, Charlie, here I come!" and "Take me out to the racetrack ." Today was going to be IT, the fast trip. I had it all planned out. If Pen said anything about me driving Charlie Stride fast, I'd just tell her he got away from me. And I'd stick to that if she tattled.

Pen was already in the barn when I got there. She had Charlie Stride out in the crossties and was cleaning out his stall. Charlie had his nose down to the yellow cat, who was smoothing around him, but

I gave a little whistle to him, and his head came up. He pricked his ears forward and whinnied to me.

"Yeah, hi, Charlie Stride," I said happily, rubbing behind his ears. "Look what I brought you." I gave him a lump of sugar, which he crunched up. Pulling his brown head down, I whispered in one ear, "Today's the day!"

He flickered the ear and nuzzled his head against my shoulder, as if to say, "Great with me, buddy!"

As I went to get Miss Loubelle D. out of her stall, I called to Pen, "I'll jog Charlie Stride."

I didn't hear her reply anything for a minute, then a little "OK" came from Charlie's stall. Penelope Greeley, meek and mild, I thought. At least she made it easier for me, not getting in my way. I gathered she hadn't told the Hartshaws about our encounter at the creek the other day, because I hadn't gotten any static about it.

We did our horse chores in uncompanionable silence until Boyd Gray came in, and then I talked with him while I put out the feed. I went over to the diner for breakfast, and I don't know what Pen did for food. Maybe she brought along some of her poison strawberries. When I came back, Pen was hitching Miss Loubelle D. to a jog cart. I went to get Charlie Stride out, and just for a second I wished I could ask Pen to watch me harness him and hitch him up, to make sure I did it right. Don't be stupid, I told myself, you've watched and helped Grandad do it plenty of times.

The colt was restless, as if my itch had gotten into him. Instead of standing quietly in the crossties, he kept moving around, pawing the dirt, shifting his haunches, rattling the bit in his mouth. "So, Charlie," I kept saying, but gently, "Whoa, man."

At last I hitched the jog cart to his harness, led him out of the barn, and we were ready. Pen and the gray mare were slowly circling the track. I waited until they were going into the backstretch, not to be near them, then I swung onto the cart and drove onto the track. Charlie picked up the trot right away, tossing his head, but I held him down to a slow jog, so that we were half the track away from Pen and Miss Loubelle D.

"Just wait, Charlie, you'll get your chance," I told him and started humming easily, the way Grandad did.

I didn't feel easy, though. I felt all nervous and squirmy inside, eager and kind of scared, too. And also I could hardly wait to speed up. The second time around the track I saw Boyd Gray come back to the barn from breakfast, and I wished Pen would hurry up and get off the track. I hadn't thought about Boyd seeing me ·speed with Charlie Stride. If Pen would just take Miss Loubelle D. back to the barn, Charlie and I could have our dash before Boyd got out there. Maddeningly, I saw the gray mare pass the track gate and head around the oval again. Charlie Stride and I followed at our snail's speed. But then the next time around, Pen guided Miss Loubelle D. off the track toward the barn. As soon as they were out of sight, I turned Charlie Stride around to go the right way, the racing direction. I shook the reins and pulled them tight.

"OK, Charlie, let's go!" I called.

And he took ahold of me. Boy, did that brown horse surge ahead! We came spinning down the homestretch and headed into the first turn, Charlie's

hooves making that beautiful steady *clop-clop*. Of course, pulling a jog cart instead of a sulky, Charlie couldn't go as fast as in a race, but the air whished past my ears. "Oh, happy day!" I sang. As we headed along the backstretch, I touched Charlie's tail with the whip, shouting, "Come on, Charlie, see what you can do!" He could do, all right. His ears laid back, concentrating, and his body streamed forward, his

clop-clop going faster and faster.

"Wow! Yeah, Charlie!" I was yelling.

This is how going fast behind Charlie feels: It feels great! Riding in a car at seventy miles per hour I never felt I was moving as fast as I did out there in the open air with Charlie's tail flaring toward my chest. And me holding the reins and feeling him move and guiding him around the turn, boy, we were a team!

Then I saw Pen standing at the fence and Boyd Gray leading his horse out of the barn. Pen's face was an open-mouthed blur as we flashed by. I began to slow Charlie, easing the reins, saying, "All right, Charlie, easy now."

I almost panicked then, because the horse wouldn't slow up. He hauled against my hold on the reins, speeding down the homestretch for the finish wire. I pulled back, and he pulled against me.

"All right, Charlie, easy!" I called over and over, my voice squeaking.

Then, with me sawing reins and him hauling, Charlie's head tossed up and down, and he broke stride. He danced around there in front of the grandstand, and then he slowed down to a walk.

"*Ne-huh-huh!*" he neighed, and he sounded mad.

"It's all right, Charlie, I'm sorry, Charlie," I kept telling him. I was panting for breath, I discovered, and the brown horse was snorting heavily, too.

I got him turned around and drove him slowly off the track. Immediately Pen grabbed his bridle.

"What in—Are you crazy?" she demanded.

Her face had come alive, eyes snapping, mouth and chin jerking. Was she mad!

"Trouble?" Boyd Gray called.

"He got away from me, wow!" I said, shaking my head.

"He did not!" Pen yelled. "You were going the right way—you were racing him on purpose!" Then, reaching to Charlie's harness, she screeched, pointing to a strap hanging loose under his belly. "Look!"

"My God!" Boyd Gray exclaimed.

"He could have caught his foot in it!" Pen cried. "He could have killed himself! Oh, Charlie!"

I began to shake. I slid off the cart, and my leg gave way under me, I was so weak all of a sudden.

"Oh, geez!" was all I could say.

Pen started to unhitch Charlie, and I saw her hands were shaking. I reached to help her, and my hand was shaking, too.

"Well, the good Lord was with him," Boyd Gray said, patting Charlie's head. "Anyway, he's all right, just lathered up. But Randy, you'd better cool it." He shook his head at me, his face serious.

Pen led Charlie Stride off to the barn, and I followed my poor horse, who was still huffing through his nose. His brown coat was lathered white with sweat.

"If he's all right, it's no thanks to you!" Pen spat at me over her shoulder.

"Geez, I didn't see the strap hanging," I began.

But she whirled on me. "You didn't see, and you didn't care!" she cried. "I saw you whip him up. I yelled to you but you were too busy hollering around the turn. You're just a crazy, careless—You don't care about Charlie—"

If she wouldn't get mad for her own sake at the creek, Pen sure could blow her top for Charlie's sake. There wasn't anything I could say. I stood there with my mouth hanging down. Charlie Stride, though, was prancing and snorting. Pen turned to the horse, and her voice went gentle right away.

"It's all right, Charlie," she soothed him down. "I'm sorry I yelled. Whoa, boy."

And so on. Pen took care of Charlie Stride, got him gentled down, and all I could do was stand there and watch. And I did, too. I watched all the time she put him in the crossties and unharnessed him and carefully wiped the lather off him. That happy brown horse, standing there all hard-worked and blowing, that horse could have been broken-legged or dead by then—because of me. I didn't try to see Charlie Stride's eyes. At last, when Pen unfastened the crossties and started to lead Charlie out the back of the barn, I spoke up.

I said, "Could I walk him, cool him down?"

"No," she said. She looked me flat in the eye, then walked away with the horse.

It was my turn to say quietly, "OK."

5

WHEN I THINK OF THE HURLY-BURLY OF ALL THOSE
county fairs and races last summer, I see fancy guys
in white suits and straw hats sitting up in the grandstands next to old farmers in bib overalls. I see shiny
new farm machinery lined up in displays next to the
grandstands—with little kids perched on top of the
combines and tractors to watch the races. I feel sweltering hot again in the midwestern sun that blazed
down on the fairground and seemed to suck humidity
from the cornfields around the tracks. I smell hot
dogs barbecueing at the Kiwanis' tent, and bacon fry-
ing at the Lions' tent, and manure steaming at the
4-H animal exhibits. I hear a country-music guitar
twanging out "Chain Gang." I hear the music and
clang of the carnival rides. I hear the *clop-clop* of the
horses racing.

But most of all, I hear the talk. Talk at the fence
rails, talk in the barns, talk over a quick meal—

county fair time was a high old time, when everybody got together for a good sociable bust-out. Mostly what I heard was horse talk, free-wheeling country talk. I noticed how Aunt Connie would broaden into a friendly drawl when she'd get to the races. At home she'd probably say, "Hi," but at the fairs, greeting people at the barns, she'd say, "How-da!" "Hidey!"

I hung around the fence rails and the barns, talking with everybody and listening to them say things like:

"My horse just hung."

"I say it's all in the bloodlines!"

"Hardest thing I ever had to do, put my old broodmare to sleep."

"Hotter'n Billy Blue Blazes!"

"Looks to me like that mare there needs a gaiting strap."

"We blazed that first part of the race awful fast."

"A pacer's a poor man's horse—takes too long to train a trotter."

"Yep, bringing along a trotter, you got to be as careful as pushing a wheelbarrow full of eggs over cobblestones."

That last was one of Grandad's statements. For all that he never seemed to talk much, he sure could come out with colorful expressions. That surprised me at first, because I'd decided that not much of anything was going on in his mind except horse training, and it was a jolt to hear him say something lively.

There was talk of the purses at the different races, how big the win-money would be, and there was talk of the big-time parimutuel tracks—"Sportsman's Park!" "Cahokia Downs!"—and the biggest race of them all, "The Hambletonian, for the three-year-old trotter!"

Asking questions, I learned the Hambletonian race happened at the end of every summer, and it was held down at Du Quoin, Illinois. It was the top honors race in the nation for the three-year-old trotter. In the same way, the big race for pacers was the Little Brown Jug at Delaware, Ohio. I asked Aunt Connie if she'd entered Scataway in the Little Brown Jug last year, and she said, "He's fast, but not that fast."

We all were in great spirits for the first fair at Mount Oak, Iowa. Aunt Connie seemed to have gotten over her cold spell toward me, talking to me—when she did talk—as easily as before. Late in the morning before the races at Mount Oak, she came into the barn, where Grandad, Pen and I were tending to the horses. Aunt Connie was carrying an old lantern and a paper sack, and she was laughing fit to double over.

"Look what the guys tied on my jog cart!" she said.

Grandad looked into the bag. "A sack of sandwiches!" he said, laughing, too.

"So what's that mean?" I asked.

Aunt Connie tossed the sack to me, playing. "It

means my horse is so slow it'll be dark and supper-time before I get him around the track," she said. "I bet it was that Carl. Will I ever make him eat dust in the first race!"

"Carl, hey?" I teased. "Is he your boyfriend? You gonna marry him?"

"Huh!" she said. "I never met a man I liked better than horses."

Grandad put in, "She goes dancing at the taverns with some of those guys after the races, though. Big waste of time."

Aunt Connie only grinned, saying, "I learn a lot after the races, talking 'em over."

That first day of races at Mount Oak was beauti-ful. Charlie Stride was to race the second day with the colts, his first big race, the Hawkeye Colt Stakes, but both Miss Loubelle D. and Scataway raced the first day, and both horses won both heats of their races.

"After the first turn, that Miss Loubelle, she just got out in front and stayed there!" Grandad said happily that night, when we had a big celebration dinner at the motel restaurant. "Never falters in her pace, most dependable horse I've ever known!"

"She's classic," Pen said softly.

"Me, I like to let the front horse break the wind for us half the race, then pull out," Aunt Connie said. She choked on a piece of salad in all the victory talk.

"You guys sure made a lot of money today," I said. "Gosh!"

I'd been figuring it out. There had been a $1,000 purse for Miss Loubelle D.'s race. Split up, half in each heat went to the first-place horse, one-fourth to the second-place horse, the rest divided between the third- and fourth-place horses. So Grandad's gray mare had earned $500 that day. Scataway's race had a purse of $750, so he took $375.

"That's $875 you've made in one afternoon. Wow! You guys must be rich!"

Grandad snorted, "Huh. Costs several thousand dollars a year to maintain one horse—feed, vet's bills, equipment, race entry fees. Plus you gotta figure in our travel, motel bills, meals. Not so rich."

"I'm just happy if my horse pays for himself," Aunt Connie added.

The talk turned to speculating about Charlie Stride's speed in the colt race the next day. Grandad was trying to decide whether to ask him to go for all he was worth. Working on the home track a few days before, he'd clocked Charlie at a new record, 2:08, remarkable for such a young colt on the hayseed circuit.

"Grandad!" Pen said suddenly. "Do you think Charlie Stride could go to the Hambletonian next year?"

Grandad and Aunt Connie were laughing and shaking their heads, saying, "Whee!"

"I don't know, buddy," he told Pen, "that's reaching for a pretty high rainbow. Charlie Stride would have to get his time down below two minutes by next

spring—and quit going on breaks. We'll just bring him along the way he wants to go and see how he does this summer."

It was a good victory dinner, talking about the day's races and making dreams about Charlie Stride. Then, after dinner, suddenly I found myself paired off with Pen. Aunt Connie went out with Boyd Gray and his wife and two other drivers, saying, "Come on now, which one of you owns a lantern that old?" and Grandad headed back for the horse barns. Pen and I followed him, but he said,

"You kids run along now, take in the carnival. Randy, you see to it that Pen has a good time. Here's some cash."

I looked at Grandad to see what he was up to, but his square face had its usual matter-of-fact look, so I took the few dollars he handed me. After all, I reasoned after my first surprise, maybe I owed Pen something. Far as I could tell, she had said nothing to the Hartshaws about my fast dash with Charlie Stride, and I guessed Boyd Gray hadn't, either. Neither of the Hartshaws acted as if they knew, although I went slinking around the next day, expecting to be scolded. I had enough punishment, as it was, because, one, Charlie kept breaking stride the next time Grandad worked him out, and two, I was sick at the way I'd endangered the horse. Much as I loved him, I was almost afraid to be around him for fear I'd do something else terrible out of my stupidity. It was a sour thing for me to realize that Pen

might be a better caretaker of that bright horse than I was. And Pen, even though she didn't say much, she knew we were in competition for the love of Charlie. Telling the Hartshaws about my fiasco would have given her the perfect chance to shut me out. I couldn't figure why she hadn't taken her chance.

As we walked across to the fairground, I asked her flat out:

"How come you didn't tell the Hartshaws about me racing Charlie Stride?"

The bright lights and noise of the carnival were up ahead, but it was dark where we were. Pen ducked her head, not answering, so I persisted, "Huh?"

Softly she said, "Nothing much to tell."

"Come on," I said, "is it because I've been letting you have Charlie Stride to yourself? Trade about?"

Her head came up at that, and a beacon from one of the carnival rides swept across her face, making her eyes sparkle.

"I don't have to wait for you to hand me Charlie Stride!" she flashed at me. "You're just a summer kid!" Then, as I was about to flash back something angry, she said, softer, "Hey, I'm sorry."

"Yeah!"

"Look," she told me, "I really am sorry, because—" She seemed to be having a hard time putting words together, as if she wasn't used to saying real things to people. "Well, because you—" she went on, "because you *are* a summer kid. You can't

be around Charlie all the time. I mean, who wouldn't love Charlie?"

"OK," I said, before it got any thicker. "Hey, you want some cotton candy? You want to go on some rides?"

It was a pretty good carnival layout, there behind the grandstand, plenty of rides, colored lights and music, plus lots of people strolling around laughing and taking chances at the ringtoss booths. Living in the city, I'd never been to a carnival, so I was ready to live it up. First we bounced around on the inflated Moon Walk and after I'd smeared on a somersault, Pen began to giggle. I'd never seen that flat girl laugh, so I did a few more crazy bounces just to see her loosen up. She laughed even more, bouncing around herself, and by the time we came staggering off the inflated plastic we were laughing together just as if we were friends. Then we went on the Ferris wheel, and as we rode up into the night above the carnival, Pen didn't shriek the way other girls would. One thing about her, she didn't seem to be afraid of anything.

"I suppose you've ridden the Ferris wheel a lot at carnivals," I said.

She shook her tails of hair. "No, no money—or time. My folks don't let me do much."

Well, that fit together. The day before, when we'd stopped at the Greeley farm to pick up Pen for the trip to Mount Oak, I'd had a glimpse of Pen's big family. I thought at the time it was no wonder Pen was so dull, because everybody in the family—parents, slabby-looking older brothers, and a swarm of little kids—seemed rather dull, as if they went along plod-plod, working too hard to talk to each other. I realized how Pen was just one of many in that family, because I didn't even notice her among the people in the farmyard until she walked over to Aunt Connie's truck. Only the mother, Mrs. Greeley, seemed something more than dull. She came across grim, the way she said to Pen, "I want you in that vegetable garden when you get back. I've had about enough of this running off to the horses."

The Ferris wheel stopped just after we passed over

the top, our seat swaying, and we sat up high there, looking off to where a rim of sunset showed against the dark horizon. It was the kind of situation where you might put your arm around a girl, so I talked, instead.

"How come you like horses, anyway?" I asked Pen.

"I don't know," she said. "Just always did." She never seemed to look at me when she spoke, except for those times when she was mad. The Ferris wheel moved, and our seat jerked down a notch, then stopped again, rocking. Pen began to talk quietly.

"When I was about eight, times were better, and we had a pony for awhile. I used to hitch him up to the wheelbarrow."

She told how she'd sit in the wheelbarrow and drive the pony with reins made of twine and pretend she was driving a fast harness horse. It made a nice picture. Maybe she told me about it because I was being friendly to her. Then, she said, her dad had to sell the pony, but after a few years the Hartshaws started letting her help with their horses.

"Your mom doesn't seem to like that," I said, "you working with horses."

"Oh—" Pen said, her voice very small, "she only wants me around when I can help."

She shut up, but I got the rest of it. Big family, too many kids—"Get out from underfoot when I don't need you." I felt more sympathetic toward Pen than I had before.

The next morning I didn't mind walking over to the Lions Club breakfast tent with Pen. There was a fine fresh feeling to the early morning, before the day's heat set in, and at the barn Charlie had seemed in fine fettle for his race that afternoon. Pen and I sat down on folding chairs around the counter under the tent. She ordered blueberry pancakes, and I ordered pancakes, fried eggs and bacon. There weren't many people eating breakfast at that time, so I noticed when a tall boy, maybe sixteen, sat down at the counter opposite us. He had a little dog with him, a white terrier, and the dog looked especially tiny because it had such a thick rope tied around its neck.

"I've got two big mouths," the boy announced to the waiter in the middle of the counters.

He ordered a big breakfast for himself and an extra order of bacon for the dog. That was neat to see, a guy's dog having a treat at the fair, too, not just eating dog food out of a can. The boy had a nice face, and I liked the looks of him.

When he said to his dog, "Great day for the races, mutt!" I called over. "Are you driving a horse?" After all, a person can get a Fair license when he's sixteen.

But he said, "None of that! I'm *riding* one. I'm a jockey."

I remembered then that the day's program had also listed flat racing, what the harness race people referred to as "running races." I talked a little with the boy while we ate, mostly about his dog, and told him "good luck at the races" when we left. Pen hadn't said anything, which was not unusual, but as we walked away from the tent, she turned to me.

"You shouldn't strike up with running race people," she said. "They're no good, any of them."

I stared at her. "What's with you? He was a nice kid."

"OK, you don't believe me, ask Grandad," she said.

So I did, when I got back to the barn. Some other guys were standing around when I asked him, and I learned in a hurry that there was a caste system in horse racing: the harness horse people looked down on the running race people. There weren't many runners at the fairs anymore, so the jockeys were a minority. Even the barn for their horses was separate, or at least, it was the last barn in the line along the track.

Grandad only said mildly, "I'd stay away from the running-race barn if I was you, Randy."

But the other men spoke up strongly. "Those guys that own runners, they're a rough lot, thieving, hard-drinking—no skill to their horse training."

And, "A running race man, he'll take what he wants and even what he don't want."

And, "I wouldn't sleep down in that jockey barn for all the rice in China!"

I couldn't believe they'd be so narrow about other horse lovers. "Ah, they're just people, aren't they?" I said.

"Not so's you'd notice," somebody grunted. To his credit, it wasn't Grandad.

I decided to find out for myself. That morning at the fence rail, watching drivers warm up their horses, I also saw a few jockeys ride horses in sprints around the track. The jockeys looked like young farm boys, some hardly older than I was. None of them seemed small and light enough to be real jockeys, just as the boy with the dog seemed too tall. Maybe they all were pretty green at riding, but there was a daredevil spirit to the way they raced those big horses down the backstretch. In some ways, flat racing looked more exciting than harness horse racing.

During a break in my morning chores, I snuck off down to the barn where the runners were. I went out the back of our barn and edged down past the house trailers parked under the maple trees. It was pandemonium in the jockey barn, compared to the quiet orderliness at our barn. Our barn even had an air of distinction to it, because some handsome spotted Dalmatian dogs hung around it. The only dog in the jockey barn was the little white terrier pup, and it's a wonder he didn't get squashed by all the men running around and horses prancing through the barn. Yet there was a feeling of fun and excitement in the barn, some loud cursing, but also a lot of joking and laughter, a lot of high spirits. I wondered if maybe the guys didn't want their horses calm and steady, the way we did, but rather preferred the racers to get geared up in the tense atmosphere.

I saw the tall boy currying a big brown horse after a sprint on the track, and I went over to visit with him.

"You gonna win?" I said.

He was down working on the horse's hind leg, and he looked up at me questioningly.

"I was at the breakfast tent, remember?" I said.

"Oh—yeah," he said. "No, I don't really expect to win. This is my first time at racing."

He seemed rather tense, although his hands wiped the horse steadily enough. Anyway, we talked, and I found out he wasn't any rough thieving joker. He was just a kid who'd moved to Iowa last winter, gotten interested in his uncle's horses, and was going to try out at racing the tall horse named Hi Dancer. The way he kept rubbing the horse's coat to a dark gloss and stopping to smooth his head, I figured he liked his horse nearly as much as I did Charlie Stride.

So, big deal, I thought, whether you ride a horse or drive him! We're all horse lovers.

I told the kid "good luck" again and trickled on back to our barn. Unfortunately, Aunt Connie, Pen, Grandad and some other drivers were out in back walking the horses, and they all spotted where I'd come from.

"Now what possible business did you have down at that jockey barn?" Aunt Connie demanded.

"Ah, I was just making friends with a kid I met," I told her, passing it off.

"Some friends you pick," one of the men said. He spat on the ground.

Behind me, Grandad said, "That boy could make friends with a fence post."

I turned quickly, but I couldn't tell from his face whether he was praising me or being sarcastic. Then, without changing expression, he winked at me. And I felt warm all over. I felt good. I do care, I realized. Even if he is shallow and one way about horses, I care what he thinks of me.

Aunt Connie was saying, "Yeah, that Randy, he'd stand there and talk to the fence post until he got it to answer back. Now if he'd just spend that much energy on learning horses—"

Pen said, "But people are important, too."

Pen was usually so quiet, it was always a surprise when she spoke up. I saw Grandad glance at her, and he kept on watching her as she went back into the barn.

Later, as I was standing at the fence rail, watching the runners line up for their start, Grandad came up beside me.

He said, "I used to jockey some when I was a youngster."

"Then you know those people aren't so bad," I picked up on it.

He only shrugged, saying, "I prefer harness horses."

I looked back to where the men were trying to get the runners into the starting gate. The way the horses kept flinging themselves around, they certainly seemed wild, some of them barely broken. Flat-race horses are supposed to go from a standing start in the gate, not moving up, the way harness horses do, but those animals were moving every which way. The owners, standing on the ground, were trying to hold their horses in the gate stalls, with the jockeys ready on the horses' backs; but the beasts kept rearing around, throwing up their heads and whinnying. One horse threw off his jockey, while the owner swore and hauled on the bridle until the horse's mouth was bleeding. There was blood all over the man's white shirt. The jockey was a game kid, though, scrambling right back onto the horse. I kept looking at the splotches of blood on the man's shirt, as he jerked around, trying to hold the frantic animal. The blood looked so violent in the midst of a happy day at the races, I began to see why harness race people might look down on the sport of flat racing, at least at county fairs. Certainly, most of those plunging half-wild horses didn't show the discipline of the long careful training that harness horses got.

Still, the boy I'd met seemed to have Hi Dancer under control. When the gate opened, the horses sprang off in a furious dash. They galloped around the track with the jockeys crouched on their backs, flailing away with their whips and yelling, and I guess it was a good enough race. But I discovered that it didn't thrill me the way the sight of a harness race did, with the drivers in their sulkies making expert maneuvers and the horses holding their heads proudly high. Anyway, I was glad to see that Hi Dancer came in a respectable third, so that my jockey friend was in the money for his first race.

I never did get to congratulate him, though, because the rest of the afternoon was taken up with Charlie Stride and his races in the Colt Stake heats. With what happened, I'm afraid I forgot all about the jockey. After the flat race I hurried back into the barn to help Grandad get Charlie Stride ready for his first heat, or at least, to watch and get in the way. When Charlie came frisking out of his stall, I just knew he'd win the race. All the time Grandad was harnessing him, the brown horse kept stamping his hooves and whuffing, as if he could hardly wait to get out there and show them all.

"Yay, Charlie!" I whispered to him. "You show 'em, all right!"

He did. He sure showed up Jake Bottle's colt, too, a big-boned black racer named Sonny Star. We hadn't seen much of Bottle at Mount Oak, because his horses were stabled in another barn. At first I was worried about Sonny Star when he set off trotting smartly beside Charlie, looking like real competition. But then Charlie Stride poured himself into the trot, stretching his legs faster and faster until he flashed past the finish wire first, with the wonderful time of 2:12. The other colts, including Sonny Star, were so far back it was hardly a race.

"Wow, Charlie! Thataway, Charlie!" I yelled.

But Charlie's second heat, later in the afternoon, was a repeat of the Athens fiasco. He broke stride. One moment he was out in front, pounding around the barn turn for the homestretch, and then he broke stride right there in front of me. He plunged his head down and broke into a gallop. By the time Grandad had pulled him aside and back into gait, the race was over. The other colts had swept past Charlie, and our glossy-brown trotter came in last. Jake Bottle's horse took first.

"Oh-h-h," Pen was moaning beside me. "He just keeps doing that! Win one heat, break the next."

"Why?" I demanded furiously. "He's a good horse! Why?"

She shook her head. "I don't know."

I remembered. My chest sucked in, I began to feel sick, and I tried not to remember it. No help. I remembered that two days after I'd run Charlie Stride fast, Grandad had asked him for top speed. And that day Charlie kept breaking stride.

"Pen, look," I said slowly. I reminded her of the time. "Look, do you think I made him bad-headed about speed? You know, racing him fast that day, and then Grandad working him hard again two days later. Would it be that?"

She stared at me with those scared blue eyes and shook her head again. "I don't know." But when I hit my hand on the fence post furiously, she said, "Probably not, Randy. Probably no fault of yours. Colts can be worked for speed two days in a row."

Charlie Stride came trotting off the track. He had his head up, snorting, and he was rolling his eyes so that they looked wild.

But it could be my fault, I thought.

"Why don't you tell Grandad?" I said angrily. "If I did anything wrong to Charlie Stride, Grandad ought to know it. Go on."

Surprisingly, Pen reached out and slapped my arm. "Randy, stop it," she said firmly. "Probably you didn't do a thing to Charlie Stride. But if you did, there's no point in telling Grandad and making a big thing of it. It wouldn't make any difference in the way Grandad is training Charlie. He's bringing Charlie along right and proper."

I looked at her steady face with the tails of hair hanging down by it, trying to sort out the truth. She turned away and walked toward the barn. I followed her.

"Are you just trying to be nice?" I asked her slim back. "You don't have to be nice to me."

"I know," she said.

6

IT WAS MISS LOUBELLE D.'S FAMOUS RACE AT CLARK City, Missouri, that brought everything to a head last summer—Grandad's trouble with Jake Bottle, my trouble with Pen over Charlie Stride, in fact, my troubles with everybody, including myself.

We'd taken the horses to several county fair races, so that it was late July by the time we went to Missouri. So far, Miss Loubelle D. and Scataway had raced very well. One time as Grandad drove Miss Loubelle D. off the track after a good race, I heard him singing softly, *"The old gray mare, she's still what she used to be!"* Of course, she wasn't really old, only eight and in her prime, for harness horses can race until they're fifteen years old. Naturally, there had been a few bad times. Just before one race, Miss Loubelle D. threw a shoe while jogging, and that meant a lot of scurrying around. Another afternoon during a race Scataway spooked at a train whistle near the track and nearly climbed the bleachers before Aunt Connie got him under control.

As for Charlie Stride, you'd just have to call him unpredictable. In one way he was keeping his promise of being a great colt, for in some races he went like a streak of lightning, as if that was the happiest thing he could do, and he didn't break stride in the second heats. But at another race he broke gait in both heats. First time out he broke before he even got across the starting line, and in the second heat he broke on the first turn in the scramble for position. I was sick that day. Sometimes it seemed as if our colt was just too nervous for the steady haul. Yet at workouts on the home track, Charlie was getting his time down toward the two-minute mile, so that we had high hopes for him in the biggest colt race of the summer. That was the Hawkeye Colt Classic, coming up in the middle of August, and this year besides the big race for the fastest three-year-old pacers, there was to be a $1,000 Greyhound Trot for two-year-old trotters. Named after the great trotter, Greyhound, of course. What's more, those races were to be run right at home at the Olden track. It was like an omen that Charlie would run on home ground. If he won that race, it would mean Charlie Stride was the top two-year-old trotter in Iowa! If only we could depend on him not to break stride.

Pen wasn't with us when we went to Missouri. Her mother had clanked down on her, saying Pen couldn't go to "every last race in the territory," that she needed Pen at home. Pen had missed two other races, too, but she still managed to spend part of every morning at the Olden track. One day I found Pen out behind the barn with Charlie. She had him following her, like a baby after a lollipop, except that Charlie—my buddy!—was following her just because he wanted to. Or at least, she had him well trained. He'd bend his long brown neck down to snatch a nip of grass, and Pen would say, "Come on, now, Charlie, come on," and he'd follow right after her. Wherever she walked, circling, doubling back, that happy colt walked right at her heels. And talking to Pen, saying, *"Whee-hee-hee!"* as he tossed his head.

I couldn't stand the sight. I ran out the back of the barn, calling, "Hey, Charlie! Hey, buddy, come here!" I tried to get him to leave Pen and come to me. The colt looked at me and whinnied, hesitating, but when Pen said softly, "Come on, Charlie," he trailed after her, looking back at me once. I stood there bluh as mud, and Pen looked at me once, also. That look, br-r-r! It wasn't a kiddish "nyah, nyah, I won" look. No, for a twelve-year-old girl, it was a very adult patient look—"Summer kid, you won't be here long."

So I didn't waste any time feeling sorry for Pen when her mother refused to let her go with us to Missouri.

It was beastly hot when we left, and then on the way down a heavy thunderstorm broke on us. The lightning was spectacular. I was enjoying it, seeing and hearing the sky go into a rage with itself, because we don't get much of that in Denver. However, the storm upset the horses. Worried that the horses might be kicking around in the trailers, Grandad and Aunt Connie pulled up by the side of the road. Charlie Stride was rolling the whites of his eyes and letting out such brays of fear he couldn't hear me talking to him at first. The Hartshaws were worried, too, about what the rainstorm might do to the track, but when we finally got there in the late afternoon, the storm had passed on, and everything was steaming nicely in Clark City, Missouri.

City, huh. More like two chicken coops and a pigsty. That's what Grandad said when I showed surprise at how little the town was, as we drove through it. He said, "Any time those old settlers got together two chicken coops and a pigsty and laid down a gravel road between, they called it a city." However, Clark City was a very pleasant old-timey-looking place. It had a town square with a sandstone courthouse, plus big trees down the few side streets and some large white old-fashioned houses under the trees. I saw people sitting out in a grape arbor next to one old house, with tall drinks in their hands, and that gave me a nice easy feeling. It was as if I'd come around a corner and found the good old days.

The fairground layout at Clark City was a good one, too. We entered under a wrought-iron gate with a sign that read, HANCOCK COUNTY FAIR, 1882.

Aunt Connie said she and Grandad liked to race there, because not only did it have a well-kept track, but the Superintendent of Speed and the other race-committee people were very cooperative, making sure everything was comfortable and fresh at the barns for the drivers and their horses. The usual fair and carnival were in progress, but we went right to the barns and got the horses settled in their stalls. By then the chores were getting to be routine for me—but not dull. I enjoyed the fact that I knew what to do in the routine, and it looked as though Grandad was beginning to trust me with the chores.

Nothing exciting happened that night, although I had a good time talking with the guys at the barn after supper. I remember I asked one fairly young man how he got started at harness racing, and he told me, "A couple of years ago I was going to buy a boat, but a man persuaded me to buy a horse instead. Hooked, now." That amused me that he'd come into the sport so casually. Usually people said they'd grown up around horses.

The one hole in the friendly atmosphere at the barn was that Jake Bottle had his horses in the stalls right across from ours. He'd been at most of the races, but always before he'd drawn stalls in other barns. Even though I went around talking to everybody, running-race people included, Jake Bottle was one guy I'd stayed away from. I didn't want Grandad to have anymore chance to associate me in his mind with that mean red-haired guy. The night before the races at Clark City he was sitting in the barn with the other fellows, and he talked as much as the rest, but there was a hard edge to everything he said. He said,

"If my horses don't race better by the end of this season, I'm going to quit the business."

And, "Only grannies race for the fun of it. Horses have got to earn their way. Takes a millionaire to support a horse nowadays."

At that, Grandad said, mild as pudding, "Yep, Jake, maybe you better sell out."

Jake Bottle glowered at him and kind of growled, "Well, I'm not giving up yet."

Early the next morning I woke up in my blanket behind the barn to hear loud voices inside. Grandad's voice cut through the morning air, saying sharply,

"What are you doing in there?"

I ran into the barn and saw Jake Bottle in Miss Loubelle D.'s stall, along with Grandad. Grandad's face had hard lines of anger, and he'd grabbed Jake's arm.

"Take it easy, Hartshaw," Jake Bottle was saying, shaking off Grandad's hold. "I was just looking for —" He stopped, and it was obvious he couldn't think what to say next.

Grandad let him flounder for a two-count, then said, "Looking for trouble. Get out of here. Don't you ever let me catch you around my horses again!"

Bottle spat in the straw at Grandad's feet. He clamped his mouth shut, shoving his sharp nose out, and walked out of the stall.

Loudly he said to another man, "Somebody ought to get the old grannies off the tracks."

Grandad ignored him, already busy checking over Miss Loubelle D. to see if Jake Bottle had done anything to her. I helped too, looking for cuts, but the horse only stood there, patient as ever, and Grandad decided his dapple gray was all right.

"Do you really think he'd try to hurt her?" I whispered to Grandad.

He replied grimly, "I wouldn't put it past him. That Bottle is a bad actor."

Since Pen wasn't there to help with the groom's chores, I was busy all morning and didn't have much time to watch and visit at the fence rail. However, I did get out there when Grandad was taking Charlie Stride around the track for his last warm-up before the races. I never got over admiring how beautiful Charlie looked as he ran, his brown coat shining in the sunlight, his legs lifting in high knee action. As Grandad brought him around the right way for a fast dash, I saw Charlie Stride shake his head almost angrily as he exerted himself.

Suddenly I wondered if Charlie liked to trot, after all. He certainly seemed to enjoy going fast, yet the way he broke sometimes and galloped, I wondered if the colt really wanted to let himself go and streak out in a gallop, the way Hi Dancer and the flat-race horses did. However, as Charlie Stride came off the track, breathing hard whuffs through his nose, he was trotting slowly, and I told myself, Sure, he wants to trot; it's bred into him. Both his sire and Miss Maybelle had good trotting records.

Charlie Stride did a fine job in his first heat that day. He didn't win, came in third, but of course, you can't win them all. Grandad and Charlie had gotten boxed in and just couldn't go. As it was, Grandad had been kind of worried that he was bringing Charlie along too fast, letting him go at speeds that weren't good for his young muscles, yet it only made Charlie Stride bad-headed when Grandad tried to hold him down.

In the next race Scataway was beaten half a length by Rocket Queen. Jake Bottle had gotten someone else to drive his mare—owners do that sometimes when they have several horses to drive in an afternoon—and the other man must have been a better driver. Aunt Connie came off the track grumpy, saying shortly that she'd cool out Scataway by herself, that I could go ahead and watch Miss Loubelle D.'s race. Therefore, Aunt Connie missed what happened at the beginning of the race, which is too bad, because there isn't a person who saw that race who will ever forget it.

It was a free-for-all for the fastest horses at the meet, and there were six horses in the race. Grandad had drawn the pole position, the number one spot on the inside fence rail. Jake Bottle was beside Grandad with a big stallion named Brown Noble, and Boyd Gray was next to Bottle with his fastest horse. As the field of horses came around the barn curve behind the starting gate, I was so proud of Grandad and Miss Loubelle D. Grandad sat up on the bike like a solid chunk under his safety helmet, his maroon and silver jacket gleaming in the sunlight; and Miss Loubelle D. was a beauty, her gray coat ashine with silver even richer than the racing silks. They looked ready for glory. On the other hand, Jake Bottle's face looked grim and pushing as he spun by, his mouth a tight line. The horses speeded up behind the starting gate, and it was as they crossed the start in front of the grandstand, and the car sped away, that everything went wild.

Jake Bottle tried to pull ahead of Grandad toward the inside fence. As he shaved close, Grandad's bike tilted a little. And for the Lord's sake, Grandad fell off! He rolled toward the fence, and thank God, he wasn't run over, as the trailing horse veered out around him. I screeched, scared to death about Grandad, but it was then that the hollering crowd began to go crazy.

Because Miss Loubelle D. went right on in the race. My eyes were following Grandad, and also I was watching from behind the horses at that point, so I didn't see what happened with Miss Loubelle D. at the moment of the accident, but later the judges said she never broke her stride. She just went right on, side-wheeling her legs in the pace.

That day, at the Hancock County Fair, Miss Loubelle D. ran a perfect race without a driver!

As they went into the first turn, Jake Bottle was in the lead on the fence, with Boyd Gray making the try beside him. Miss Loubelle D. raced behind Bottle on the fence, still hauling the empty sulky. Then as they came out of the turn, Boyd Gray, who was still on the outside, fell back a little, and Miss Loubelle D. pulled out. Down the backstretch she raced beside Brown Noble, moving up the lead horse. On the turn in front of me, she ducked in behind Bottle again to hold the number two spot, just as if she could hear Grandad saying, "Now let the lead horse break the wind awhile, Loulie." All the way around for the second half of the mile, Miss Loubelle D. held the number two spot on the fence behind Jake Bottle, until the horses came out of the last turn. Then she whipped past Boyd Gray, who had fallen back, and pulled up beside Brown Noble until they were neck and neck down the homestretch. That gray mare stretched her legs, stretched her long neck out, ears back, and she streamed ahead at the finish wire. Miss Loubelle D. had won the race!

That track roared like its lid had blown off. I was shouting, "Whee-boy! Miss Loubelle! Hurray for Loubelle D.!" Aunt Connie had run out when the shouting began, and she was jumping up and down like a six-year-old kid. Hats were sailing in the air. And the people in the grandstand and bleachers were hoorawing as if they'd been waiting all their lives for such a happy holler. Nobody had ever seen anything like it. Throughout the race, amid the shouting, I

heard snatches of the announcer's voice on the loud-speaker squawking, "Folks, you won't believe this—" and "Now she's moving up the lead horse—" and "superb pacer—" and "doesn't need a driver!"

Which was silly, that last. Miss Loubelle D. had turned in a performance that was a testimony to the perfect training she'd had from Grandad. Confidently, intelligently, the gray mare had made exactly the right move at exactly the right speed at

every point in the race. And that was it: she was utterly dependable, our dapple gray. I don't think there's another harness horse in the world who could have done what that mare did. Maybe she couldn't do it, either, time after time, but Miss Loubelle D. did it that once.

As the horses slowed and wheeled in the first turn to parade back past the judge's stand, the announcer was saying excitedly,

"I don't know how the judges will figure out this race, don't know how they'll call it, but we'll take 'em as they ran."

And he greeted each driver as he came past the stand, the last horse coming back first, "Thank you, Mr. Jones, thank you, Mr. Gray—" Jake Bottle had come in second, so it was, "Thank you, Mr. Bottle." And then came Miss Loubelle D. That smart old mare, she knew she'd won, and she'd waited to parade by last for her honors. Head up and turning a bit from side to side, she paced slowly past the grandstand, pulling the empty sulky.

Scream! Oh wow, how that crowd loved her and cheered for Miss Loubelle D.! I felt as if my heart would bust right out of my chest.

Once, during the race, I'd looked again for Grandad and had spotted him in the center field, yelling with the rest of us. He was gripping his right shoulder with his left hand. Then, as Miss Loubelle D. paraded in triumph before the crowd, he ran around the fence opening at the quarter stretch and chased after her, still gripping his shoulder. "Yay, Hartshaw!" went the crowd. He caught Miss Loubelle D.'s bridle, and I saw him take her head in both his hands. Aunt Connie and I were running down the homestretch toward them by then, dodging the horses coming off the track. I don't know what Grandad said to his gray lady, but then I heard his voice speak loudly to the judges' stand.

"Mr. Judge, I would like to register a complaint."

Immediately the watching people hushed down. However, Grandad didn't say anything more for public consumption. He turned to me and Aunt Connie, breathing heavily and gripping his shoulder again. "You're hurt—" Aunt Connie began, but Grandad looked at me, blue eyes fixing me.

"Randy, you take Miss Loubelle D. back to the barn. Take the best care of her you know how," Grandad said.

I knew I had never received a more solemn order, and I nodded.

To Aunt Connie Grandad said, "You come with me," and he called after me, "Send Boyd Gray up here."

Then, as the crowd watched and waited, Grandad and Aunt Connie mounted the steps up to the white wooden perch that was the judges' stand.

Talk about glory! That was the closest I came last summer to personal glory, when I climbed into the sulky behind Miss Loubelle D. As the people whistled and yelled again, I drove that fabulous mare down the homestretch and off the track toward the barns. For a second I knew what it was like to be a winner, and my head buzzed. I loved Miss Loubelle D. I'd never driven her, and that time, even though she was lathered and tired, she moved like silk sliding against the reins.

In front of the barn I unhitched her from the sulky.

She was breathing hard, but her gray head was still up, proud. I rubbed her muzzle, looking her in the eye.

"Miss Loubelle D.," I told her, "you're a queen!"

She watched me, her gray ears flicking forward at my voice, and then, the final beauty of the day, she rested her nose down on my shoulder. I knew, for sure, she was a gracious queen, and she'd forgiven me.

But as I led her into the barn, the trouble part of it all began to hit me, and I quit being happy-excited and started being worried-excited. Lots of people ran to pat the wonderful gray mare and congratulate her, but there was a buzz of talk about the accident and was Hartshaw hurt? And what was going on in the judges' stand? Also from the talk, I found out that although Miss Loubelle D. had run a spectacular race, she couldn't win. To win, the horse must have a driver in the sulky. So there was confusion about how the judges would call the race. But maybe they'd call it a race, and Jake Bottle would be the winner.

I saw Bottle at Brown Noble's stall, a few men talking to him, and suddenly I thought, I ought to punch him in the face! I was sure he'd shaved too close and bumped the wheel on Grandad's sulky. He'd sure been out to get Grandad today. Maybe he'd caused the wreck deliberately. And if Grandad's arm was broken, I thought, what would that do to his race plans for the rest of the summer? I felt sick and mad. There were so many mean things spurting up that I wanted to snarl at Jake Bottle, I couldn't sort them out.

Just then, however, I saw Boyd Gray and told him that Grandad wanted him at the judges' stand. While I was speaking to him, the announcer called on the loudspeaker for Mr. Jake Bottle to come to the judges' stand.

I concentrated on taking care of Miss Loubelle D. the very best I knew how. I watered her carefully at intervals, sips of water; I wiped the lather off her with cold water and gave her legs the little osteopathic rub that Aunt Connie had shown me; I blanketed her, and I walked her behind the barn. At that time, the horse people at the barn—drivers, wives, grooms—were chattering about the wreck and saying some rough things about Jake Bottle, once he was gone. It was more than taking sides with a newly famous horse; people just naturally seemed to like Grandad Hartshaw and dislike Jake Bottle. I'd seen that before. As they waited for an announcement from the judges, people got to telling about other wrecks they'd seen or had been in. Harness horse people always refer to an accident as a "wreck," even if the accident is getting kicked by a horse. They were saying,

"I walked right over that horse in the wreck."

And, "the bike flipped over the horse."

And, "put her foot right through the bike wheel."

I listened, still keyed up, but underneath I kept worrying about Grandad's arm. Once I'd learned that Queen Loubelle couldn't be declared the winner of the race, I didn't care how the judges called it. All I cared about was whether Grandad was hurt.

Once I'd put the gray mare into her stall—she never had needed as much cooling out as Scataway required—I went over to Charlie Stride. He was edgy with all the excitement in the barn, and I probably didn't help any, rubbing his neck and enthusiastically telling him what a great race he'd missed seeing. But when the brown colt began gyrating around in his stall, whinnying and kicking a little, I realized I should calm down for his sake. I talked soothingly to him, "So-o-o now, easy, Charlie," and when he came near the stall gate, I caught his head and rubbed it slowly and steadily to gentle him.

Then I heard the loudspeaker blaring, and I ran out of the barn to hear what was going on. I caught something about Brown Noble being the winner and "hearing tomorrow." Some people in front of the barn filled me in: The judges had called it a horse race, and that made Jake Bottle the winner, since Grandad couldn't qualify. However, Grandad had officially called a foul against Jake Bottle. The next afternoon a hearing would be held to decide whether Bottle was guilty of interference. If he was guilty, he'd be disqualified, and the third horse across the finish wire would be declared the winner.

"But what will happen to Bottle?" I demanded.

They ought to put him in jail for ten years, at least, I was thinking.

"If he's guilty, $100 fine or suspension from racing for fifteen days, or both," the man told me.

"He's guilty, all right!" I said.

I wanted to run up the track to join the Hartshaws and see how Grandad's arm was, but it did occur to me that I ought to stay with our horses. Somebody should be with them, to make sure there was no more trouble that day, I thought, and Grandad would come to see his mare as soon as he could. So I went back to Miss Loubelle D., gave her another sip of water, and checked the other horses. Soon enough, Grandad and Aunt Connie came down the passageway through the barn, nodding and answering briefly to all the people who wanted to talk to them. Grandad was still holding his shoulder.

"Is your arm broken?" I called to him.

"Don't know," he said. "How's Miss Loubelle D.?"

She leaned her nose over her stall gate, whinnying to him, and I left him alone to talk with his fabulous mare.

Aunt Connie told me, "His shoulder may be dislocated. We're going to the hospital for X rays."

Her eyes shone vivid brown, her face was pale, despite her tan. Both she and Grandad looked as if they were in shock. Boyd Gray came along and said,

"Come on, I'll drive you to the hospital."

I stayed with the horses, so it wasn't until that night at supper that I heard the whole story. By then we knew that Grandad's shoulder wasn't dislocated, although it had gotten a terrific pull in the tangle. With his firm grip on the reins, Miss Loubelle D.'s power had been pulling him forward as the bike threw him sideways. His shoulder was badly wrenched, and the doctor had told him not to drive a horse for a week or more, if Grandad wanted that shoulder ever to be strong again.

"What a time to have a lame wing!" he groaned.

The Hawkeye Colt Stake Classic was less than three weeks off, and Grandad and Aunt Connie had planned to take the horses to two more meets before then.

"I'll drive," Aunt Connie told him. "Don't you worry, I'll drive them all. Or maybe Boyd Gray will help. Maybe he'll drive one of the horses next week at Hooper."

As for the wreck, Grandad said he'd seen Jake Bottle's sulky coming too close, and he had tried to veer away, but Bottle's bike wheel had hit Grandad's wheel just as he'd veered. That's why the bike had tipped.

"He had no business that close!" Grandad declared. "He bumped me on purpose!"

So he had formally called a foul against Bottle.

"Serves him right!" I said. "Now you'll get him!"

Grandad only shook his head. "Who wants to fool with a skunk? I wish I didn't have to have anything to do with Bottle, wish I didn't have to race on the same circuit with him. But he's dangerous, and they ought to get him off the tracks."

"OK," Aunt Connie said. "Now let's talk about Miss Loubelle D."

We told each other again exactly what neat things the gray sweetheart had done at each point of the race—"did you see how she—," "steady as steel—," "I couldn't believe it when she—." People stopped by our booth to ask about Grandad's shoulder and congratulate him on his mare. One driver's wife said she knew somebody on the staff of a horse magazine, and surely the man would want to write up an account of Miss Loubelle's miraculous race. Aunt Connie said she was going to write it up herself and send it in.

Well, the hearing went all right the next day. I thought Jake Bottle should go to prison, at least, which of course, he didn't. But the judges did find him guilty, finally. The hearing went on a long time, for the judges went over the points and testimony carefully. Jake Bottle acted very surly and defensive, insisting, "I just drove where there was an opening. Hartshaw panicked. He veered away from me and tipped his bike over, himself!" Grandad, on the other hand, was his most stolid and unemotional. "I felt the wheels bump," he said. Boyd Gray testified for Grandad, saying that he was surprised when Bottle pulled over so sharply, because Bottle wasn't that far ahead of Hartshaw. He admitted, upon questioning, that he didn't actually see Bottle's wheel touch Hartshaw's bike, but he said he heard a scraping sound. Jake Bottle had not been able to get any witnesses to speak in his defense. One of the judges, too, said he'd seen exactly what had happened, "and it certainly looked like interference to me."

So Jake Bottle was found guilty. Brown Noble was disqualified from receiving any winnings in that race. Bottle was fined one hundred dollars, and he was suspended from racing for fifteen days.

I figured out that meant he'd miss the next races, but he could race again by the time of the Greyhound Trot at Olden.

Outside the hearing room Grandad made to leave without looking at Jake Bottle. However, Jake said loudly, "Some justice, when they blister a man just because an old granny can't sit up in his bike!"

He was so mad his face was redder than his hair, and I think he would have punched Grandad, except that then he'd only have been in more trouble with the judges.

Grandad turned and spoke straight at Jake Bottle. He said, "We'll see who can drive when we get to the Greyhound Trot."

7

"CHARLIE STRIDE LOVES ME!"

"No, he likes me best!"

"But see how much better I take care of him!"

That's the way it went for the next couple of weeks. We didn't actually say those things, but the feeling was there. Pen and I seemed to be on a see-saw over Charlie Stride, first one of us up, then the other.

At first I was up, because while Grandad was out of commission for driving, he gave me the job of jogging Charlie Stride. Boyd Gray had agreed to give Miss Loubelle D. her stiff workouts in the late mornings and to drive her in the next two races. For the rest, the Hartshaws decided that Aunt Connie would take care of Scataway plus do the hard workouts with Charlie Stride to ready him for the Greyhound Trot. That left Pen and me to do the slow jogging. Pen would drive the gray mare, and I drew Charlie. Pen was at the barns even more than usual, because Grandad went to her mother and explained that he really needed Pen's help until his shoulder healed. I think he persuaded grim Mrs. Greeley by offering some pay for Pen's time.

Grandad was really unhappy that he couldn't be getting in solid work with Charlie Stride before that big race, and he went around muttering to himself for a couple of days. But Aunt Connie was good with our colt, too. She had a fine sense for feeling him out when he was getting headstrong or about to break. And she scolded Grandad that if he expected to drive Charlie in the Greyhound Trot, he'd better take care of his shoulder and let it heal. To relieve Grandad's shoulder, after the hearing at Clark City, Boyd's wife had driven one of our pickups home, hauling the horses. Nevertheless, the next day Grandad was so sore he could hardly move his arm. The first few days back at Olden he was taking pain pills, soaking in hot baths, and resting his arm in a sling. A few times in his muttering I heard, "Bottle!" as if he were grinding the name between his teeth.

I felt sorry that Grandad was in pain, especially since the pain made him grouchy, but I couldn't help being glad at the way things worked out to give me a chance with Charlie Stride.

The first morning back at Olden, Pen was at the barn, and Grandad told her to take Charlie out for his first round of jogging. So actually she was up on the seesaw first. I thought bitterly, That's the way it's going to be: Pen, the right-hand man! She's got more experience.

But then Pen ran into trouble. Grandad was standing by the fence rail, coaching Pen, and he called out for her to let Charlie Stride speed up a little. I could see she was pleased because she'd never done anything but slow jogging with Charlie. But as she speeded him up, he took the bit, broke stride and began to gallop. When I saw Pen whipping along in the jog cart after Charlie, I was a little scared for her. She had an awful time getting the powerful horse back under control, and in fact, she didn't really, because Charlie Stride finally slowed down only when Grandad yelled at him as he came around the track again. When Pen drove off the track, her mouth was pulled in a straight line, as if she were mad, but her eyes were watery.

Grandad said, "You gotta eat more potatoes and gravy, buddy, get more weight on you so you can hold this horse."

He said it jokingly, but Pen took a gulp of breath, and I thought she was going to cry. She didn't, only gasping out something about, "yeah, need more weight."

It was true. At twelve she was just too skinny and light to haul back on Charlie Stride when he started acting up. Grandad eyed me, and I was glad I had a solid body, shaping up to be stocky, because my extra weight won the chance for me. The next trip out that morning he told me to take Charlie Stride.

It was an all-around bad day for Pen, I guess. First thing when we'd met at the barn, naturally we'd told her all about Miss Loubelle D.'s perfect race, all of us talking. Her eyes were bright blue, hearing about it, but at the end she said sadly, "And I didn't get to see it!" Grandad had been kind to her, saying, "OK, buddy, you take Charlie out now," but then she'd messed up on that, too. Afterward Grandad told her, "Come on, you help me take care of Miss Loubelle D.," and he arranged that she'd slow-jog the fabulous gray racer for the next week, but I doubt if that made up to her for the disappointment.

Still, when I got out on the track with that prancy brown horse, I forgot about feeling sorry for Pen. It was clear that Grandad seriously expected me to be responsible for Charlie's slow jogs. Grandad rode around on the cart while I drove, and for the first time he began to give me in-depth coaching about driving Charlie Stride.

"Keep your shoulders solid and steady—no, not tense—your power comes from your shoulders, not your wrists. . . . That's right, let your wrists be flexible. Yeah, but strong. Don't let Charlie feel like the bit is fluttering in his mouth. OK, now let him speed up a little. . . . Now slow him down, show him he's got to obey you."

And so on. Even for slow-jogging, all of Grandad's coaching was designed to train me to feel the horse, and for the horse to feel me. Which was exactly what I wanted. Boy, was that what I wanted! I was concentrating so hard on learning from Grandad and feeling the horse, that I didn't realize how happy I was until we drove off the track.

"Grandad!" I said, sliding off his lap. "That was great! Thanks a lot!"

He only nodded. "Tomorrow you can try it alone."

I think Grandad worked harder that week than if he had driven Charlie Stride himself, what with coaching me and coaching Boyd Gray with Miss Loubelle D. Later that first morning Boyd Gray took the mare out to get used to her, and by the end of the morning he got Miss Loubelle D. up to some speedy dashes. At first Grandad watched closely, too, when Aunt Connie took Charlie Stride out for the heavy work, but she was well acquainted with Charlie's tricks, so there was no problem there.

"Only trouble is," Aunt Connie said, smiling but shaking her head, "Scataway will get jealous of Charlie Stride."

She stood in the passageway between the two horses, who were in stalls across from each other. Charlie Stride whickered his happy call to her, whereupon Scataway reached his brown-black nose out over his stall gate and butted it against Aunt Connie's shoulder. She threw her arm around Scataway's neck, saying, "It's all right, Scat."

I'd never seen Aunt Connie love over her horse the way I made over Charlie Stride, patting him and talking to him. She simply concentrated on Scataway. So he seemed to notice that she was taking

Charlie Stride out that morning and the mornings after, and he resented it. Once, when the horses were both out in the passageway, Scataway danced his hind hooves sideways and tried to nip at Charlie's haunch. Aunt Connie decided then that she wouldn't go near Charlie in the barn, leaving all the groom's work on Charlie to me and Pen. Which suited both of us, of course.

While I was up on the seesaw over Charlie Stride, it was easy for me to be nice to Pen. One day, as we cooled him out after I'd jogged him, I talked to her again about Charlie's tendency to break stride and gallop.

"Do you think Charlie Stride really likes to trot?" I asked her.

She smoothed down Charlie's sleek nose, looking at him, not me. "I don't know," she said, playing her usual dumb shy routine.

I persisted. "But is it bred into him that he'd *really* rather trot than gallop?"

Finally she answered me, "Horses don't really want to run at all. Unless they're scared. I read that."

She glanced at me, and I gave her my best reassuring "go on" look. So Pen went on telling what she'd read in the book, that basically a horse is a herd animal, and his primitive instinct is to stay in the middle of the herd, racing away only to escape a wild beast. Horse races and getting out in front in a race are a man's idea, not the horse's.

"See, a horse is making a sacrifice to race at all,"

Pen said. She was back to looking at Charlie Stride, scratching him behind his ears. "He just races to please his master."

"Ah, Charlie likes to run," I protested. "You know that. He likes to kick up his heels and move fast."

"Well, yes, but Charlie's unusual," she said. She held up the bucket for him to slurp water. "He's got so much spirit, as if running is fun."

"So," I said, getting back to the original question, "does he think it's fun to trot? If so, why does he gallop?"

"Oh, don't be so stupid!" Pen said suddenly. "Naturally, if Charlie Stride is trying hard to win a race, it's easier for him to gallop than to stay in a schooled gait. Sure, he has the tendency to trot, but still, he's making a sacrifice to stay in the trot when he's trying to move fast. It's discipline. Look, I'll lend you the book, if you want."

"Thanks," I told her. But I didn't want to learn about Charlie Stride from a book, when I could spend every day with him.

Those were wonderful mornings, working out with Charlie, and he seemed to enjoy them as much as I did. Every time I came down the passageway, he stuck his head out of his stall and called to me with his friendly whinny. Whenever I opened his stall gate to take him out, he nibbled on my arm and made soft sounds in his throat. We were learning to feel each other out very well in the jogging sessions. The times he broke stride I pulled him down, and he always picked up his gait right away.

Something great was happening between me and Grandad, too. We were in it together, jogging Charlie, and Grandad treated me like a partner, like a sensible human being, not a nuisance of a kid. He'd stand by the fence, watching me and the colt, sometimes calling out a bit of advice, and when he'd say, "That's right, now you're doing it, buddy," it felt like big praise to me, and I'd sit up a little straighter on the jog cart.

I didn't spend any time analyzing and thinking Grandad was shallow, all one way for the horse. I was too tired by night to think about it, anyway. I didn't mind that he hardly ever called me by name, Randy. "Buddy" was good.

Then one morning Grandad told me to turn Charlie Stride around the right way. He said I could take the colt for a little dash, though not too fast, he cautioned. Wow, did I light up! But only for half a minute. I tightened the reins, touched Charlie up with the whip, and we started speeding around the track. Yet just as I was beginning to feel glory-bound, *ker-clop,* Charlie broke stride. We were going into the first turn, and maybe I wasn't handling the reins right—anyway, he broke into a gallop. I sawed him to a stop, feeling awful. One minute you're sailing along, all happy and excited, building up, and the next minute, *zoom,* you're way down at the bottom, out of the race.

It reminded me of the first time I'd tried to race Charlie Stride, the time I'd run him with a broken strap. Suddenly I couldn't stand hiding it any longer. If that brush was the thing that was making Charlie bad-headed about speed, then Grandad ought to know about it. The brown colt was snorting and pulling his head, wanting to do *something.* I turned him around and jogged him slowly back to where Grandad was standing by the fence.

I knew then why I hadn't told Grandad before. Deep down I was still hoping he'd like me. And news like this probably would put the kiss of death on my chances.

But if hiding the facts meant Charlie would never

prove up as a trotter—

I got off the jog cart and held Charlie's bridle while I told Grandad about that day. When I got done, he just looked at me, his face not revealing anything.

"I know," he said. "Boyd Gray told me the next day."

I stared at him, at his unyielding silence. Suddenly I was furious. He could have yelled at me right away, as soon as he found out from Gray, and we'd have had it out in the open. But no, he'd gone on all this time, thinking who knows what about me, just keeping silent about it. Even now he wasn't going to reveal any reaction to me.

Angrily I said, "Well, is that what's making Charlie break?"

"Didn't help," he said.

Another silence. I turned to lead Charlie back to the barn.

Grandad said, "Randy, it didn't take you to teach Charlie Stride his tricks. He's still a colt, hasn't learned all his good patterns yet."

I looked back at Grandad, eagerly. But that was all the comfort I was going to get. His face was the same, still concealing whatever he really thought of me. I sighed.

"OK. I'm sorry," I told Grandad.

Obviously my confession wasn't going to make any difference to Charlie's training, just as Pen had warned me. And it was no relief to get it off my chest, when Grandad had known my secret all along, no telling whether he forgave me or not. That feeling of partnership with Grandad—maybe it was just in my mind.

I took Charlie Stride back to the barn.

The next day something worse happened. It was the day before we trailered the horses over to Hooper for the races. I came into the barn to check on Charlie, and I thought I'd left everybody out at the track. But I heard a kind of *snick* sound in Charlie's stall. I had walked in quietly, for once, and she didn't hear me coming. Pen. I saw her in Charlie's stall, leaning up against the brown horse. She had her face laid on his side, and I saw tears trickling down her cheeks. Even crying, she was silent, only making that *snick* sound as she sucked in breath. Charlie Stride was whuffing softly at her. He turned his head back and lipped her shoulder as she leaned on him. Without looking at him, she slid an arm around the horse's neck. He kept on lipping and nuzzling her shoulder.

I turned around. Grandad was standing in the passage, watching, too. Both of us went out quietly, and neither of us said anything.

That afternoon I walked through the pasture and down to the creek. It was a heavy afternoon, heavy with heat and haze, the sky dulled by thin heat clouds. It was hot down at the creek, too, but at least the mud in the creek bed was cool under my feet. The creek was so low in August that I could see the rocks on the bottom of the pool where Pen had sat fishing.

I'd never seen her down there at the creek since that time. As I eased down on the big rock, I wondered if I'd run her off from the creek, too.

Oh shoot, I thought. It wasn't as if I'd permanently taken her place with Charlie Stride, just because I was getting to jog him. I'm just a summer kid, I thought, like Pen said. I'll be gone by September, and she'll have him all to herself again. Why worry, just because a girl cries over a horse?

Or a grandfather? Only she would never have leaned up against Grandad and cried. Well, why shouldn't he spend time with me? He was *my* grandfather! I dashed my foot against the little bit of water in the pool and watched the ripples spread.

Aw, but shoot! Who likes to see a girl cry? And not even crying to get something, to manipulate somebody, just crying all by herself.

But Grandad *wanted* me to jog Charlie Stride. What could I do about it? Even if I went to him and offered to let Pen do it, I could imagine him saying, "No, the horse comes first." Pen wasn't strong enough yet to do the job.

It just wasn't fair. Not in the area of human beings. I thought that, being as factual as the stone I'd picked out of the water. I hefted it in my hand, noting the solid reality of the smooth stone and its wetness. This stone is a fact, I thought, and Pen's feelings are a fact. It wasn't a matter of being sorry for a girl because she'd cried. She'd put a lot of herself into Charlie Stride, a lot more than I had. So she had a right to a solid relationship with Charlie, maybe even a right to jog him, even if she couldn't always do it the best. "The horse comes first," I thought. Always? Don't people ever come first?

That night as we finished up supper—watery scrambled eggs and thick chunks of bacon, Aunt Connie's idea of a light summer supper—I said to Grandad,

"Let's go look at Sister Belle. Just you and me."

Aunt Connie raised her eyebrows at that, then shrugged.

Grandad was always glad to go out and make over the foal, so he came along. It was generally late when we ate supper, after doing the end-of-day chores with the horses, so that the sun had gone down. The day's heat was softening into evening, the sky hazed with pinkish-gray clouds over in the west. A meadowlark gave its last calls, sweetening the air. Miss Maybelle and the foal were down at the far end of the pasture toward the creek, so we had a way to walk and talk. I noticed how heavily Grandad stumped over the rough ground and around manure piles, as if he were tired. His arm wasn't in the sling anymore.

"How's your shoulder feel now?" I asked.

"Lot better. Should be able to drive soon."

I plunged into it. "You saw Pen crying today."

"Yep."

I didn't know how to go at it next. "Well—it's not fair. I mean, me jogging Charlie all the time. Oh, I want to, but—Pen's got a right to Charlie, too."

"Not right now, before the Greyhound Trot."

There it was. *The horse comes first.* But I wanted more from my grandfather. I wanted him to show he was a man who could see more than one rigid rule of thumb. Out of justice I knew Pen had a stake in Charlie, but I was even more concerned about my stake in how Grandad acted then. Pen had been his friendly buddy all along. If he would do something to show he cared about Pen's feelings, then I'd know he cared about people, too. Not just horses. I'd know he could care about me. Whether I was good with horses or not.

Sister Belle came running up the pasture to greet us. She was beginning to have a body to go with her gangly legs, not a baby foal anymore.

"Look at that!" Grandad said happily. "Pacing! A natural pace to her. Yessir, Sister Belle." He caught her head and rubbed the brown muzzle.

He's not going to say anything more about Pen and Charlie, I thought. He's just going to let it go.

Furiously I said, "Yes! She'll make a great filly, too. And she'll have problems, and you'll work them out. There'll always be another colt and another horse. But Grandad! There's only one Pen! She's a human!"

He turned to me, his face stern in the graying light. "Randy," he said, "I don't know what you're making this fuss about."

I tried once more. "Grandad, listen. You know what Pen is like. You know what her family is like,

150

all those people not paying any real attention to her.
Grandad, Pen needs Charlie. She needs that horse!"

He looked at me. "So?"

"So let her jog him, whether it's good for Charlie
or not."

There, I'd said it. Heresy.

Grandad's little blue eyes didn't give anything
out to me. He sighed, absently fondling the foal's
neck.

"Go on back to the house," he said finally. "I don't
want to talk anymore."

I turned and ran through the dusk up the pasture,
not even caring when I stepped *splosh* in a manure
pile. I took deep even breaths to keep from sobbing.

OK, I thought. Some people just haven't got it. Grandad is who he is, and that's all he is.

I went to bed that night, and the last thing I thought was, He's no grandfather to me.

The next day when we drove the horses to Hooper, I didn't talk to Grandad anymore than I had to, but I was extra nice to Pen at the fair. I walked around the 4-H exhibits with her, looking at the ram and the pigs; I took her on the rides at the carnival; I even bought her a souvenir of the Hooper fair, a hand-braided belt. Helping guys in the barns at previous races, I'd earned a few bucks, and I spent it all on Pen. I don't think any of that helped. The thing about Charlie Stride must have been eating her, deep down, because most of the time she walked around as if she weren't really seeing the things in front of her. However, once when we came back into the barn, she was smiling over a horse joke I'd just repeated to her, and Aunt Connie saw. When Pen went back to Charlie's stall, Aunt Connie swiped her hand across my head, ruffling my hair.

"Glad to see that redhead finally gave in, made friends with Pen," she said.

"Sure," I said easily. Let her think what she wanted.

Yet I knew that Pen and I still were rivals over Charlie Stride. Early in the morning before the Hooper races, I took Charlie out on the track for a jog. As I drove him around the track with the dew still damp on the dirt, I couldn't help being proud of

Charlie, knowing people were watching him and speculating on that speedy colt they'd heard about. I brought him off the track still trotting smartly, a little too fast for coming into the area in front of the barns, and nearly ran over a spotted dog. A man called out, "Slow down there, Barney Oldfield!" but it was all fun, part of the excitement that builds up every morning before the races. Charlie was full of himself, prancing gaily as I led him into the barn. I rubbed his nose, "Getting yourself all nerved up for your race, huh, boy?" and he whuffed happily, "*Whee-ha-ha!*"

Then I saw Pen leaning against a stall, chewing on one of her tail ends of hair, just watching me and Charlie. She didn't jump to help me unharness him, just let me have Charlie Stride all to myself.

"Here," I said, "you take him, OK? I got to do something."

She looked at me suspiciously but took Charlie's bridle.

Grandad was in Miss Loubelle's stall. I saw him glance at us, his face bland as always.

Old dish-face, I thought. Shallow as a plate. Too bad Pen isn't a horse. Then he might give a damn about her.

That afternoon Charlie Stride pulled his same trick. He won the first heat in wonderful time, then broke stride in the second heat. I was watching, wondering if he really was making a sacrifice to race in a controlled trot. Right then, as he pulled out of the barn turn into the stretch drive, Charlie shook his head and broke into a gallop, as if to say, "I want to run! I want to play it my way!" Immediately Aunt Connie pulled the colt up, and Charlie obeyed, went back into his trot, but he finished last, of course.

At the barn afterward, Aunt Connie said, "He's still a baby. He still wants his own way, wants to play."

"He's got to get over that!" Grandad said.

I couldn't help sympathizing with the colt, even though I wanted him to win. After all, he was only two years old. Why shouldn't he be full of high spirits and play?

The morning after we got back to Olden, I heard a funny sound coming from Charlie Stride's stall. It was a *rattling* and a *whanging* and a *bump-bumping*. When I saw what it was, I started laughing. That colt! He was playing with an empty bucket. He'd lift it with his snoot and toss it, run after the bucket and chew on it, rattling it, then switch around and give it a little kick with his left hind hoof, for all the world like a kid flipping a ball into a basket backward.

"Hey, Charlie!" I said. "Come on, you want to play?"

The Hartshaws were still out in front unloading equipment from the pickups, so I led Charlie Stride out behind the barn. We had us a little more horseplay, playing tag. I raced around, and Charlie wheeled after me, trying to nip me. When he'd catch me, I'd tousle his head, and he'd whinny happily.

It was there that Grandad found us, and it was then that he came down on me harder than he had all summer.

He stood at the back opening of the barn, calling, "Randy!" When I noticed him, I had the feeling he'd called before.

"Come over here," he said abruptly. "All right, Randy, I want you to stay away from that horse. You're not good for him."

"What?" I stared at Grandad, trying to see his features against the dark opening of the barn, after the sunlight in my eyes. "Hey, just because we're playing a little—"

"Too much play," he said. "Too much excitement. You're nerved up all the time, and you keep Charlie Stride keyed up too much. He's nervy enough, as it is."

"But—but—" I felt as if I'd been dashed off a hilltop.

Grandad went on, laying it out in a flat voice. He said Charlie Stride needed to settle down and work, if he was to perform right at the Greyhound Trot. I was to stay clear away from the colt until after the Trot. In a few more days, he said, he should be able to drive Charlie himself. Meantime, Aunt Connie would jog Charlie, and Pen was to take care of him at the barn. Pen was to do all the groom work for Charlie Stride.

When he said that, I saw Pen behind him in the

darkness of the barn. In the duskiness, her face looked startled and shining.

"Huh!" I said. Some new ideas came at me. "Huh!"

Was he really doing this for Charlie's sake, I wondered. Or was it for Pen?

"OK!" I said.

And I grinned at him.

For once, Grandad looked surprised.

8

WHAT A WOW OF A POSITION I WAS IN, MAYBE THE worst of the whole summer. And maybe I'd put myself right there. I couldn't help laughing at myself, shaking my head, as I walked around the side of the barn. But then my head went down, when I tried to sort things out, so that all I saw was rocks and clods of dirt and the toes of my sneakers, kicking at them. It looked as though Grandad had listened to me; he was giving Pen her chance. So I should feel good: my grandfather did care about people! But caring, doing this for Pen, where did he leave me? Out in left field again. "Stay clear away from Charlie Stride. You're not good for him." Was he just saying that to help Pen? No, I thought, he meant it. Maybe he was doing something for Pen, but he meant it about me and my nerviness, too. The worst of it was, I kept worrying that maybe he was right.

OK, I decided, I'll play it his way.

Besides, what else could I do?

The rest of that day, wherever Charlie Stride was, I wasn't. The Hartshaws didn't work the horses that day after the Hooper races, only slow-jogged them a little. When Charlie was on the track, I did a few chores in the barn. When he was in the barn, I watched the other horses on the track. I didn't get to drive any of the horses, because Aunt Connie jogged them all. When the Hartshaws went back to the barn late in the afternoon to give the horses their evening feeding, I stayed at the farm.

The next day the Hartshaws turned Miss Loubelle D. over to me for her slow-jog workouts. I tried to take pleasure in driving her, in feeling the smooth sure way she paced, but I wished she were Charlie, frisking and trotting. Later, I stood at the fence rail to watch him when Aunt Connie gave him a strong workout, and as Charlie came by, he turned his head to look at me. He did it again the next time he came around.

Aunt Connie stopped him and called over to me, "Stay away from the fence, or go up in the bleachers if you want to watch. He keeps looking for you."

I went back in the barn, but I felt good, anyway. Charlie kept looking for me. Maybe he missed me! Then when Aunt Connie brought him back into the barn, I was still there. Charlie danced his hind legs around and tugged away from her, whinnying to me. He came up to me, lipping my arm and whuffing, "Hey there, Randy, where you been?"

Ah, Charlie.

I felt so warm in my chest, and I was grinning and rubbing his head. But I saw Grandad looking up from examining Miss Loubelle's leg, looking at me and the colt.

So I said, "Yeah. OK," and turned away from the horse, left him to Pen. She was there, waiting to take over with him, give him his rubdown. She gave me a worried look and kind of raised her shoulders, but I went on out of the barn.

She followed me when I was dragging myself up to the bleachers to watch. "Look, I'm sorry," she said. Her plain face was wrinkled up with worry.

"Forget it," I said, hard. "Probably Grandad's right. Probably you're better for Charlie than I am." I turned my back on her so she'd go away.

Still, something great happened in those few days. I found out that Charlie Stride really did like me. He was such a friendly colt that I'd never known whether he liked me any better than the barn cat, just another of his buddies. I'd felt sure Charlie loved Pen more than he did me. But those days while I was staying away from him, he started whinnying in his stall, not happy whuffles, but long loud neighs, calling. Pen would go in and calm him down, but soon he'd start calling again. Once when I happened to be in front of the barn as he came off the track, he rushed up to me, dragging the cart, and made happy whimpers as he butted his head against me. Then I could believe it: Charlie cares. Charlie misses me!

It helped, while I was staying out in left field. In fact, it made all the difference. I could believe that someday Charlie Stride and I would get back together again.

While I was staying on the edges, I kept watching Pen and Grandad to see whether he showed any more awareness of her. So far as I could tell, he treated her about the same—"Come on, buddy, let's go to work." Yet that seemed to be all it took to make Pen happy. When Charlie was on the track, and I was in the barn, I'd watch them, I'd watch my grandfather and that skinny girl working together, unharnessing Miss Loubelle D. and rubbing her down, neither of them saying much, maybe Pen handing Grandad a brush or both of them bending down to examine a stone nick on the mare's leg. And they were perfectly happy together. I tried to imagine Grandad saying to Pen, "I'm sorry you have a rough time with your family," or "You're a nice girl," and I knew she'd run like a rabbit.

So Grandad and Pen were getting along fine in their own way. And I felt like an extra left hand.

Mainly Grandad concentrated on Charlie Stride in a big push to get him ready for the Greyhound Trot. He started a strict work program for Charlie; the idea was to teach the colt not to break stride in a dash. Every morning Charlie slow-jogged the first time out. The second and third workouts of the morning he jogged briskly; and then at the end of each workout, he was turned around the right way for a fast mile. Grandad was trying to get Charlie to run two heats a morning without breaking trot. And each morning he asked Charlie for a little more speed. He clocked the mile carefully, starting with a fairly slow speed the first morning, the mile in 2:20, the next morning in 2:16, and so on. After the first day of workouts, Grandad took over driving Charlie Stride himself.

"This old wing is ready to fly again," he said.

He admitted his shoulder was sore after the first day's workout, but he left Miss Loubelle D. to me for jogging and to Aunt Connie for the faster trips, and after a few days his shoulder didn't bother him any more.

When Charlie went out on the track for his fast workouts, I tried to be up in the grandstand to watch. I'd watch intently as he turned around the right way for the big try, watch Charlie's knee action as he came past me, watch his body race around the backstretch, listen for the steady *clop-clop* of his hooves as he came around the barn turn. When Charlie would make his second try of the morning, my chest would feel pinched, I was so tense, watching and listening. If the colt couldn't make two dashes in a morning without breaking, then probably he couldn't complete two heats of a race.

Grandad noticed me up in the grandstand, and the second day of the fast workouts he gave me an extra stopwatch. He said I should help clock Charlie's time. He had made both 2:20 dashes the first day without breaking, now he was going to try for 2:16. The first mile Charlie made it, right on the button for time. I clicked the stopwatch as he crossed the finish line, and I wanted to yell "Great!" but I kept quiet. The next time, later in the morning, Charlie went around in his same smart rhythm. As he came into the homestretch, I glanced at the stopwatch, and—oh, my heart thudded—I heard Charlie break. *Clop-clop* broke into *ker-clop, ker-clop.* I saw Grandad stop him and jog slowly back the wrong way on the track. Then he called up to me,

"Gonna try it again. Just a half mile, 1:08, this time."

He jogged Charlie around the track the wrong way once and turned him around by the barns. There they came again the right way past me. I gripped the stopwatch, breathing steadily, "Come on, Charlie, come on, Charlie."

And he did. Flashing bright brown in the sunlight, our colt did just fine. He raced around the track and came speeding past the finish line right on the nose at 1:08 for a half mile without breaking trot. As Grandad brought him back toward the barn, Charlie tossed his head happily, as if he was glad he'd done it, too.

I could hear Grandad praising him, saying, "Sure, Charlie! You can do it. Good boy!"

But the day after that, when Charlie did two heats in 2:14, it was even better. Because when he made his second dash of the morning without breaking stride, Grandad called to me as they slowed up past the finish wire.

"Get down here!" he called.

I jumped down out of the grandstand onto the track, falling over myself.

"Give him a pat," Grandad told me.

Wow, would I ever! But I remembered that stuff about my nerviness, so I didn't run to my sweet bay colt all jumping and yelling. Solid and steady I walked up to his head, hugged his neck and rubbed his nose firmly.

"Good boy, Charlie! You did it!" I told him, looking him in the eye.

His bright eyes flashed as he bobbed his head at me and whinnied, "Sure did! Ain't it grand!"

Maybe something else was grand. It was beginning to seep into my thick head: with Grandad, it really was "show," not "tell." Maybe in his own way he was showing me that I could be his buddy.

I couldn't hug Grandad, and I couldn't roughhouse with Charlie, so that night I let off my steam when Aunt Connie and I were doing the dishes. The dirty dishes and pots had stacked up for a couple of days, and we were having a real go at them. I started jigging around the kitchen with the dish towel, singing, "*Camptown racetrack, five miles long!*" And I let out the dish towel in a zing, snapping Aunt Connie on the hip.

"Hey!" She turned around, laughing.

"*Doo da! Doo da!*" I danced around zinging at her

again, and Aunt Connie gyrated, trying to get away and laughing, "Hey, cut it out!" At last she got me smack in the face with her wet washrag. It was fun, teasing her, the sure way to get her to loosen up and laugh. Actually, I think Aunt Connie was glad for a chance to let off some steam, too. As we went on doing the dishes, we sang together, *"Somebody bet on the bay!"*

Anyway, from then on, I was Charlie Stride's reward every time he made his fast mile without breaking. I guess Grandad had noticed that the colt seemed to be looking for me and missing me. And Charlie learned fast. It only took one time, when he broke on the 2:10 try, for him to find out I wouldn't appear and praise him when he fouled up. I don't know whether my part helped, or whether it was all due to Grandad's patient steady work, but Charlie was down to a 2:06 mile without breaking by the time we went to the races at Egger's Landing.

Was I happy! I was still staying away from Charlie except for those proud moments at the ends of his dashes, but I felt I was part of his training.

And at Egger's Landing, the work program proved out. Grandad didn't allow Charlie Stride to go too fast in the competition, but instead made the colt obey him, keeping a steady pace so that Charlie came in third in both heats at 2:16. Jake Bottle was in the races at Egger's Landing. His track suspension was over, and he was back to driving again, but he was very silent with the guys when I saw him in front

of the barns before the races. When his big colt, Sonny Star, took first, though, he was hollering and laughing as he drove off the track, and for a minute I almost liked Jake, he acted so kid-happy. But later in the barn Jake called some smart remark to Grandad, and Grandad didn't pay attention, didn't even look at Bottle. Grandad had accomplished his purpose, to race Charlie two heats in competition without breaking, and that was all that mattered. It was the final test before the Greyhound Trot.

The Hartshaws let the horses rest the day before the Hawkeye Classic races at Olden. In the morning Grandad and Aunt Connie were busy helping the local race committee on last-minute details: making sure fresh hay was brought in and that the stalls were clean in the other barns for the visiting horses. Then, when the Hartshaws gave our horses their noon feed, and Charlie kicked his stall gate, and Aunt Connie snapped at him, she came out of the barn, saying,

"Come on, let's get out of here for awhile. Let's go over to Sheffield Park."

Now, that just goes to show: the Hartshaws had never even mentioned Sheffield Park before, and it was a neat place to go, too. We got some barbecued chicken and potato salad at the grocery store, and all of us climbed into the pickup, Pen and I in the back. Probably Mrs. Greeley wouldn't have let Pen come along, but Pen just came, anyway.

"Mom knows I have to help today and tomorrow," she said.

We drove about twenty miles to a little country park, where there were lots of big oak trees and limestone cliffs along a small brown river. The main feature of the park was the Indian mounds, three grassy humps nearly as high as a one-story house.

When I saw the mounds, I said, "What kind of an Indian name is 'Sheffield'?"

Pen said, "Well, that was the name of the man who found the mounds."

"Poor Indians," I said. "Also-ran to Sheffield."

We had the place nearly to ourselves, just one family with little kids in the other end of the park. After we ate our chicken and potato salad, sitting up proper at a picnic table, the Hartshaws stretched out on the grass to nap. So Pen and I went over to climb the Indian mounds. Sure, that's what you always do with Indian mounds.

"Hey, down there," I called into the hump. "How's eternity?"

Pen said primly, "He's not down there, he's in heaven."

She scrambled up the hump after me, and we sat on top and talked a little about what kind of Indian could have been buried there, and why the big mounds were made. It was easy to speculate, because Pen didn't know anything about it. I wondered how Pen did in school. She didn't seem to know anything about anything, except horses—and maybe people.

We could see Grandad and Aunt Connie lying on

the grass with newspapers over their faces, probably asleep.

"They needed to get away, get some rest," Pen said. "Connie may not show it, but she's awfully tense about Charlie Stride."

"We all are," I said. "But look," I went on, exploring it, "what would happen if Charlie doesn't win? Or if he breaks?"

I knew how I'd feel, but we had to face the possibility, and I wondered how real horse people would look at it.

"Well," Pen said slowly, "We'd all feel bad, really bad. If Charlie doesn't come in first, well, that could happen just because some other colt is in better shape tomorrow. But if Charlie breaks—" She shook her head. "It could mean he's in a pattern that's terribly hard to change."

Of course, Grandad would keep on working with the colt, she said, hoping Charlie would shape up finally for his three-year-old season next year.

"But if he keeps breaking," she said, pulling up grass, "maybe we'll just have to face it: he's not willing to train as a trotter."

I thought of the bay colt floating around the track, long legs reaching down to check the ground in perfect rhythm. I remembered his precise knee action in some of his dashes. If ever there was a beautiful trotting horse—

"He's a trotter!" I insisted. "We know he is!"

Pen sighed. "Well, we'll see what happens tomorrow." Then she looked up at me and grinned. "OK, you keep believing that. Every little bit helps!"

When we got back to the Olden track late in the afternoon to give the horses their evening feeding, the place was beginning to swarm. Some of the visiting horses and drivers were already there, and more trucks were driving in. Horses were stamping out of trailers, people were calling to friends, "*How*-da there!" and already there was the smell of supper cooking in some of the little house trailers back under the trees. Horses whinnying and snorting, horseflesh everywhere, people running around like kids at a circus—I mean, it was exciting!

We didn't see anything of Jake Bottle at first. Grandad had asked the race committee not to quarter Bottle's colt in the same barn with ours. I heard some talk about Jake, though, and it gave me a slightly different view of him than I'd learned from the Hartshaws. Some guys in the tack room were talking about Jake, saying he was about to go broke on the horses. Jake didn't have financial backing, and his horses weren't winning enough purses to support them. I remembered Jake had said something about that himself, down at Clark City, before the races. I fooled with some harness, listening to one man say, "Sorry situation. The more Jake Bottle thrashes his horses to win, the more they lose." The other guy said, "Yeah, pretty desperate man. Too bad."

Curiosity took me snooping until I found Jake Bottle and Sonny Star in the third barn down. The Classic and the Trot were for colts only, so he didn't have his other horses with him. From the back of the barn, I watched as the red-haired man settled the black colt in his stall, shoving Sonny Star around as if he were a piece of furniture.

How could any colt be a winner with that kind of treatment, I wondered.

Yet as I watched, Jake stood still by the horse, rested his hand on the horse's head, and just stood there, looking at Sonny Star. It was different to see Jake Bottle so quiet, his narrow face set in those hard lines. He looked down and very human. But it was no use feeling sorry for Jake Bottle right before the

Greyhound Trot, so I got away from there before he saw me.

We took Pen home and went over to another neighbor's farmhouse for supper. It was a gala pre-race feast, food set out on long tables, picnic-style, and lots of out-of-town visitors dropping in. There was plenty of talk and laughter, and Aunt Connie laughed, too, but she looked revved-up, brown eyes sparking. Grandad looked the same as ever, his comfortable square face chuckling with some old-timer buddy. After we ate, he took me and Aunt Connie home. He was going to sleep at the barns with the horses, he said. I wanted to go with him, but he said,

"Nope, you keep Connie company."

Aunt Connie didn't seem to want to go in the house. We wandered around to the remains of Grandma's vegetable garden and picked a few stray spears of asparagus and ate the heads raw. Then we walked down in the pasture and talked to Miss Maybelle and Sister Belle, who were feeding gently at grass in the early dusk. Aunt Connie laid her cheek against the foal's muzzle.

"I'm so wrought up it's a good thing I'm not driving tomorrow," she said. "Though I might feel better if I were."

"What's the matter? Don't you trust Grandad?" I was uneasy suddenly. But her tone reassured me.

"Sure," she said. "Might as well not trust the Rock of Gibraltar."

We didn't speak of Charlie Stride and whether

we could trust him.

Aunt Connie studied the sky, where dark clouds were rising in the west. "Hope it doesn't rain tomorrow," she worried. "That's all we need, a muddy track."

We'd had very little rain that summer, almost a drought, so I hadn't seen Charlie Stride perform on a really sloppy track. At last we went to bed. Sometime in the night I heard thunder and then rain on the roof. As I roused, I thought about Aunt Connie and wondered if she were lying in bed with her eyes open, listening to the rain.

It was still raining a little when we woke up, but when we got to the barn, people were bustling around, saying cheerily, "Rain before seven, shine before eleven." Sure enough, the sky was clearing by the time we fed the horses and went for breakfast. The track was already starting to steam with the day's heat, but a little breeze had come up that might cool and dry out the air. I had wondered if Grandad had been rained on, sleeping behind the barn, but he looked cozy and dry when we got there. He said he'd slept in the tack room, no problem, except that the other fellow in there snored. Race day might make Aunt Connie tense, but Grandad seemed even more at ease.

I saw him freeze-up cold later in the morning, though. I was standing by the fence, watching the horses warm up, including Charlie, when Jake Bottle walked by. At the same time Grandad came driving Charlie off the track after a good brush.

Jake Bottle said loudly, "Oughtta call that colt Break Stride, from what I hear. Just hope Granny Hartshaw can control him, so he don't foul up the race."

Grandad didn't look at Bottle, but his face was set and cold as he unharnessed Charlie from the jog cart. Pen helped him, and she copied Grandad, not looking at the man. But I stared a hole in Jake as he walked on, seeing his sharp nose and lined face. I thought, Jake Bottle, you really make it hard for a guy to like you!

That morning the usual buildup of excitement before the races was intensified, because all the horses racing that day were rompy young colts. There were the three-year-old pacers for the Hawkeye Classic and the two-year-old trotters for the Greyhound Trot. Both races would be run in two heats. However, there were quite a few more pacers than trotters, so the pacers' first heat would be run in two sections. The lesser number of trotters competing reminded me again that it was extra-special to train a trotter, and I felt proud of Grandad and Charlie.

But once, when I looked down the line of stalls in the barn, I saw Charlie chewing splinters off the post of his stall. I wondered how nervous he was getting. Maybe chewing on things calmed him, I told myself.

At last it was 1:30 in the afternoon. The track had dried out pretty well, the tractor-drawn scrapers had gone over and over the dirt to smooth it, crowds of people were gathering in the grandstand, and the sun blazed down out of a clear blue sky. Race time!

The first race was a heat for pacers in the Classic. We watched at the fence in front of our barn as the three-year-olds went swaying by. I liked the style of a certain neat brown mare, and I was glad to see her take first with a good time of 2:10. The next heat was another section of pacers. Horses that can run in a pace tend to go a fraction faster than trotters, but I didn't see anything spectacular in that race. The brown mare's time was still the best. While we were watching, Grandad left us to go back in the barn to Charlie. Pen came out of the barn, where she'd been staying with Charlie, and stood with me and Aunt Connie. The next race would be the first heat of the Greyhound Trot.

When Charlie trotted out onto the track with the other colts for the warm-up sprints, suddenly my stomach churned so hard I thought I was going to throw up. I glanced at Pen, wondering if she'd heard my stomach rumble. I was glad I wasn't driving that alert brown colt, or he'd sure feel my panic. But Grandad looked as if he had every one of his nerves under control, sitting up there in the sulky as steady and chunky as if that were his natural home, as if he slept, ate and bathed in a bike behind a horse. When Charlie and Grandad spun around the track, a lot of people in the grandstand yelled, "Yay, Hartshaw, yay, Charlie!" Charlie Stride was the only trotter from Olden in the competition, so naturally, he was a hometown favorite. Charlie tossed his mane as if to say, "Sure! Watch my dust!"

The announcer blared away on the loudspeaker, and the horses pulled into their lineup position in the backstretch. The starting gate car picked them up, and they came sweeping by us in formation, a beautiful field of seven horses and drivers. Jake Bottle and Sonny Star were in the number three spot, and Grandad had pulled the number five position in the drawing, so Charlie was way back there after they crossed the starting line, but he started picking up speed. When the colts came out of the first turn into the backstretch, I saw Jake Bottle had pulled in along the fence behind the lead horse, and Charlie Stride was racing on the fence behind him.

Geez, Grandad, I thought, don't get boxed in! They held those positions as they came by us, with the number four horse challenging the colt in the lead. I ducked back suddenly, in case Charlie would look for me, and I didn't start yelling for him until he was in the backstretch again. By then, boy, was he doing his stuff! He'd pulled out beside the lead horse, racing neck and neck, body stretching. The number four horse had faded back, and Jake Bottle was still in the number two spot on the inside fence.

As the horses came pounding by us on the barn turn, I ducked down and watched past Pen's legs. It didn't matter; Charlie Stride wasn't looking for me. His ears were back, and he was concentrating on getting out in front, knees flashing. Out of the turn, he did pull in front, and that's all boys! Charlie dashed down the homestretch as if he was headed for supper. Half a length ahead and first over the line!

"He didn't break!" I yelled. I grabbed Pen and danced her up and down. "He didn't break! He didn't break!"

"He won!" she was squeaking.

Sonny Star didn't break either, although Jake Bottle hollered and thrashed the black back with his whip all down the homestretch. Then the loudspeaker called Charlie's time: 2:08 for the mile.

"Hurray!" Wow, did that crowd shout! We all yelled and hurrayed. What a great time for a two-year-old trotter! "Hurrah, Charlie! Hurray, Hartshaw!" people yelled when finally they paraded last past the judges' stand.

Aunt Connie just kept shaking her head and grinning and saying, "Oh, boy! Oh, boy! I don't know if I can stand another heat."

It's a good thing we had an intermission then, while the Olden high school band played and we all bought pop.

When Charlie came trotting off the track, I hugged his head, saying, "Great, Charlie! Good old Charlie!" and he whuffed on me, but I stayed away from him in the barn. It was Pen who went to help Grandad unharness our great trotter and cool him out. While I was waiting in the push of people at the pop stand, I felt lonely. Of all days to be left on the outside, away from my brown buddy—yet, I thought, this is my sacrifice for him. At that, I had to grin at myself. Sacrifice, huh. Big deal. Lately I'd been concentrating so much on Charlie Stride and his training, I hadn't had room to think about myself.

Well, whatever, I thought, right now he's excited enough without adding my excitement. Now Charlie needs to calm down. For that second heat, he's *got* to be steady. It didn't really surprise me that Charlie won the first heat. I remembered Grandad saying happily, races ago, "He wants to race, all right!" But when it came to the push in the second heat—

Later, though, watching that neat brown mare win the Hawkeye Classic, I kept thinking about me and Charlie. Was I *always* to stay away from him because we were both excitable? Surely, as he got older and more dependable, and as I did—Aw geez, surely Grandad didn't expect me to stay away from Charlie Stride forever. He couldn't!

Suddenly I realized something that I'd managed not to think about. In two more weeks I had to go back to Denver for school.

A cloud came from nowhere to cover the sun, and I felt cold and miserable as the colts trotted out onto the track for the final heat of the Greyhound Trot. Then I felt somebody clasp my hand, and it was Pen, standing there beside me.

"Remember, Randy," she said, "you keep believing he's a trainable trotter. Keep believing he won't break." Her eyes were intense blue.

"Sure," I said, trying to smile. "You, too." I tugged

one of her tails of hair.

The colts were lining up behind the starting gate. Quickly I looked to pick out Charlie Stride. He was in the number one slot next to the fence, having won the first heat, and Sonny Star was outside in number three again. In formation they speeded up to the starting line, and they were off, hooves pounding, bike wheels spinning.

What a race that was! I think I could set off in a rocket for the moon and not feel as scared and happy

and roiled up as I did during that race. That time Charlie kept his lead, running in front all the way around to the barn turn. As I saw him coming, I breathed, "Oh, Charlie, Charlie, you're a trotter, don't break!" As they flashed by, I saw Grandad's lips moving, talking to Charlie, too. "Heeyuh!" Jake Bottle hollered behind them, number two on the fence by then. His eyes looked black. I couldn't tell what happened in the shuffling on the turn past the grandstand, but then in the backstretch Jake Bottle

made his try. Sonny Star pulled out from behind, and my heart thumped as I wondered how close he was shaving Grandad's bike wheels. But Grandad shot along, solid as ever in the sulky. The big black colt pulled up on Charlie, and when they came into the barn turn, they were side by side. Sonny Star didn't lose ground, even though he was on the outside.

I didn't duck down, I couldn't move, as they pounded by. I saw Grandad flicking the whip on Charlie's haunches, leaning forward just a little, and I could imagine him saying, "That's it, Charlie, come on, boy." But Jake Bottle was yelling and whipping his colt, urging him into the lead.

Suddenly, as Charlie turned into the homestretch, I saw him strain forward as his head bobbed once. *Oh, Lord God,* I thought. For sure, I thought he was going to break.

But it was then that I saw how it works: Whatever a person is, that's what he puts into his horse.

Charlie steadied. I couldn't tell what Grandad did with the reins or what he said. But Charlie's legs never broke rhythm. He stayed true to his training. *Clop-clop* went on steadily, and *clop-clop* speeding faster, as that brown horse let out another link, slim legs reaching faster and faster in the trot. A nose ahead of the black colt, a neck ahead . . . Bottle bellowed "Yuh!" whaling with his whip . . . and Sonny Star broke gait!

A second later Charlie Stride flashed over the finish line!

I just stood there with my mouth open.

"He didn't break!" Pen squeaked beside me. "He won!" She sat down, plop, on the ground.

At last I could give a long let-out happy yell. "Yay-y-y, Charlie! Hurray-y-y-y-!"

Our horse had come in first!

"You know something?" I squatted down to Pen on the ground. "You know what? Our horse came first, so our horse came in first!"

She only stared at me and giggled. Because what could a person gabble except silly things in excitement?

But, it was no time for philosophy! I raced after Aunt Connie, who was running down to meet Charlie Stride and Grandad. Pen came running after us. So we all—all of us from Belleview Stables—took the bow with Charlie Stride when he came parading in front of the grandstand last, the position of honor. Charlie pranced for the cheering crowd until Grandad brought him to a stop in front of the judges' stand. Pen threw her arms around Charlie's neck, as he stood stamping and blowing. But I ran up to Grandad.

"Sir," I said, sticking out my hand, "it was—beautiful." I began to stammer. "Con-congratulations!"

He pumped my hand, chuckling, his blue eyes blinking at me. "Yeah, yeah, it was beautiful!" Even he was breathless.

Then the judges gave Charlie Stride's time. It was remarkable. "Two-Oh-Four!" Two minutes, four seconds for the mile.

At last I got to hug Charlie, too. His hot brown neck was slippery with lather, his mouth full of slobber, but I didn't care. I don't think I've ever been happier in my life than when he blew on my ear with that soft soft mouth of his.

Except maybe the next moment, when they brought out the winner's blanket, and Grandad let me put it on Charlie's back. As I draped it over him, he looked back, eye bright. I smacked his neck, "Sure, Charlie, you and me!" And he gave a sudden snort, lifting his lip in a grin, "Sure, Randy!"

Well, when I think of that race, that's the last high moment. The rest of the summer runs into a happy blur. Grandad didn't talk to me anymore than before, but I could begin to believe he trusted me, so I chattered away to him anyway, until he'd say, "All right now, shut it down." But then he'd hum, and I'd grin. Grandad raced Charlie Stride only one more time that season, and our steady colt didn't break then, either, although his time wasn't so spectacular. However, the last two weeks were just a solid happy time for me and Charlie. Grandad let me help take care of him and jog him again, so I tried not to roughhouse with him too much when the colt and I were feeling frisky. If I did, Pen just looked at me with those quiet reproving eyes of hers. And Pen and I managed to share Charlie OK.

It was no pain, sharing, and not such a pain, parting in September, because the last week I was there,

Grandad told me the best news of all. Out at the professional horse racetrack in Denver, where they'd always had running races, they were going to start having harness horse racing, too, early this winter. And the Hartshaws had decided to bring their horses out. So,

"See you next winter, buddy!" Grandad said.

I can hardly wait. He and Aunt Connie will only be here for a two-month season, and Grandad said he didn't expect to race Charlie Stride very much, the colt still being young for the parimutuel tracks. But I'll get to see that happy brown horse at the barns nearly every day for two months. And again next summer, and the next—until I'll be old enough for my driving license. After all, horses can race until they're fifteen years old. It'll be a few years, but Charlie Stride and I are going to race together someday!

Glossary of Harness
Racing Terms

Backstretch—straight stretch at back of track opposite grandstands.

Bay—brown; horse can be light bay or dark bay.

Bit—steel part of bridle inserted in horse's mouth for control
of horse.

Bike—nickname for sulky, because fitted with bicycle wheels.

Blinder bridle—bridle with shields on sides so that horse can
see only straight ahead; required for horses that look
around too much.

Break stride, break gait—break into a gallop instead of holding the run to a trot or pace.

Broodmare—nonracing mare of good bloodlines kept for pur-
poses of bearing foals.

Brush—a short spurt of running at high speed.

Checkrein—rein running from the bit in horse's mouth to top
of head, then back to hook on harness; causes horse to
hold head high. When head is up, a more balanced stride
is achieved.

Cheeked his bridle—controlled horse's head by holding bridle
by horse's cheek.

Clocking time—a stopwatch is used to time speed of horse down to seconds; watch can be clicked to start and stop on the second.

Colt—one to three-year-old horse.

County fair circuit—harness races at county fairs, nonbetting races; generally run by less professional horses.

Crossties—ropes or chains extending from stalls; fastened to horse's halter or bridle, they hold horse in position while being harnessed or groomed.

Curry—to comb a horse's coat with a currycomb; more generally, to groom a horse.

Dapple gray—patches of darker gray on silver gray.

Drawing for position—for the first heat of a race, drivers draw numbers for their starting position.

Field—a racing group of horses and drivers in sulkies.

Finish wire—wire stretched above track, generally from grandstand to judges' stand; marks start and finish of race.

First turn—first curve of oval track after the starting line.

Flat race—running race; racing of horses ridden by jockeys.

Foal—newborn horse, one under one year old.

Founder—in horses, to go lame because of excessive water or feeding.

Gait—manner of moving the legs and feet: walk, trot, pace, canter. Schooled gait—trained to run in a trot or pace.

Gaiting strap—strap from bridle along side of horse to sulky; used to keep horse's head straight ahead.

Gallop—natural run in three-beat gait; also canter.

Gelding—a castrated male horse.

Harness racing—racing horses hitched to sulkies and driven by reinsmen sitting on sulkies.

Heat—one course in a race. A harness race generally is run in two or three heats. Winning horse of the first heat starts in the No. 1 position in the second heat, second-place horse in No. 2 position, etc. Horses may win portions of the purse on each heat.

Hobbles, hopples—leather or plastic straps encircling the front and rear legs on the same side to keep those legs moving in unison while pacing.

Homestretch—straight stretch to finish wire in front of grandstands.

Inside rail—fence around the field in center of oval track.

Jog—slow run in trotting or pacing gait.

Jog cart—similar to sulky but heavier, easier-riding.

Judges' stand—generally a high platform mounted at the start and finish line, often placed at edge of center field opposite grandstand.

Mare—female horse.

Pace—lateral gait; right front and back legs going forward at same time.

Parimutuel tracks—professional horse-racing tracks where people may bet money on the races.

Parading horses—driving at slow speed past grandstand to show off horses.

Parked out—forced by position of other horses to travel on the outside of the circle around the track, thus covering more ground.

Peekaboo bridle—round blinds that fit over horse's eyes adjusted exactly so that the eyes are in the center of the opening.

Pole position—No. 1, in front on the inside rail; generally considered most desirable starting position.

Purse—sum of money offered for winners of each race; first four placing horses in each heat divide winnings of the purse.

Racing silks—fancy jackets worn by drivers, distinguished by their personal color combination.

Sawing reins—pulling reins back and forth alternately.

Shadow roll—sheepskin-type roll worn below the eyes, restricting view of track; worn to prevent shying at objects.

Standardbred—American breed of horses bred for trotting or pacing.

Starting gate—metal wings mounted on an auto, a barrier to keep horses in line and prevent them from getting ahead of the starting gate; controlled speed of auto brings field of horses up to proper speed by the time they cross starting line.

Sulky—light vehicle consisting of two wheels on an axle, seat for the driver and poles extending to the horse's harness.

Tack room—room in barn or stable where harness and other equipment are stored.

Trot—diagonal gait in which left front leg and right rear leg move forward at same time.

Trot the mile—on a half-mile track the horse goes around twice.

Winning the blanket—a fine horse blanket is given to the horse with the best time in any heat of the race.

W-line—rope tied in a W from horse's front legs to back legs, for purpose of training horse not to rear in harness.